TOGETHER, APART

"Love, Delivered" copyright © 2020 by Erin A. Craig
"The Socially Distant Dog-Walking Brigade" copyright © 2020 by Bill Konigsberg
"One Day" copyright © 2020 by Sajni Patel
"The Rules of Comedy" copyright © 2020 by Auriane Desombre
"The New Boy Next Door" copyright © 2020 by Natasha Preston
"Love with a Side of Fortune" copyright © 2020 by Jennifer Yen
"The Green Thumb War" copyright © 2020 by Brittney Morris
"Stuck with Her" copyright © 2020 by Rachael Lippincott
"Masked" copyright © 2020 by Erin Hahn
Cover art copyright © 2020 by Liza Rusalskaya

All rights reserved. Published in the United States by Delacorte Press, an imprint of Random House Children's Books, a division of Penguin Random House LLC, New York.

Delacorte Press is a registered trademark and the colophon is a trademark of Penguin Random House LLC.

Visit us on the Web! GetUnderlined.com

Educators and librarians, for a variety of teaching tools, visit us at RHTeachersLibrarians.com

Library of Congress Cataloging-in-Publication Data is available upon request.
ISBN 978-0-593-37529-7 (trade) — ISBN 978-0-593-37530-3 (ebook)

The text of this book is set in 11.5-point Adobe Caslon Pro.
Interior design by Andrea Lau

Printed in the United States of America
10 9 8 7 6 5 4 3 2 1
First Edition

TOGETHER, APART

Stories by

Erin A. Craig · Auriane Desombre
Erin Hahn · Bill Konigsberg
Rachael Lippincott · Brittney Morris
Sajni Patel · Natasha Preston · Jennifer Yen

DELACORTE PRESS

CONTENTS

Love, Delivered

by Erin A. Craig

"This is it!" Mom said brightly, opening the door to my new room with a grand, ceremonial swing.

I stepped over the threshold, eyes wide as I took in the high arched ceiling, the oak window seat, and my lamp—a bust of Edgar Allan Poe I'd made in ceramics class, already assembled and looking hopelessly out of place against the stark white walls.

You and me both, buddy.

"What do you think?" Dad asked, coming up behind us. "Just a second," he called down to one of the guys from the moving company.

"This is it," I echoed, trying to muster enough cheer to appease them.

"Do you like it?" Mom asked, pushing back one of the

curtains the previous owners had left behind. It was some sort of floral chintz and would be coming down the second I was alone. "We were going to wait and let you pick for yourself, but then on the tour—this just screamed *Millie.*"

It *was* a cool room, I couldn't deny that.

It just wasn't *my* room.

But it was now, I supposed, no matter how I felt.

Mom and Dad were both scientists. Researchers who specialized in viral pathology. Mom had gotten a pretty sweet job offer at the University of Michigan, working in the hospital labs during the summers and spending the rest of the year as a professor. Dad was going to stay at home while he worked on writing his first book. Some dry textbook he swore would be in freshman biology classes all over the country.

Not a fun book, like the thrillers and mysteries I read.

I'd never seen them so excited before.

We were supposed to leave Memphis in May, allowing me to get through school and still spend part of the summer with my friends, getting to do all our favorite things together one last time. I'd have June, July, and August to settle in and hopefully meet some new friends, just before senior year would start.

But then COVID-19 broke out and literally everything fell apart.

I didn't finish the school year. I didn't get one last concert or film festival, no last Grizz game or barbecue nachos, no cupcakes from Muddy's bakery.

I didn't even get to say goodbye.

Our house—our *old* house—already had an offer on it, with most of our stuff packed away into boxes and bins when the governor closed the schools, then the stores, then the state.

"Stay at home?" I remembered shouting at my parents with an anger completely uncharacteristic of me. "How do you stay at home when we *have* no home?" I'd burst into tears and run up to my room before they could answer.

Mom and Dad had talked late into the night, their furtive whispers filling the house. I could hear them wondering what to do, wondering if they were making the right decision, wondering how we'd get through any of this.

Less than twenty-four hours later, everything was decided for us. The hospital in Michigan wanted both Mom and Dad working there. Pronto.

In the blink of an eye we were supplied letters certifying that my parents were essential, pledging that our movers were essential, swearing up and down that the new house was essential.

Everything was essential but my misery.

"The light is different here," I said, feeling both sets of their eyes on me now, their concern as heavy as the semi truck parked along our drive.

Our lane, as my father insisted calling it.

Back in Memphis we hadn't had a driveway. Now we had a lane. Of our own.

A lane and a garden and a little old supply shed, painted barn red and outfitted with scalloped white trim.

There was no way to deny it. We were country now.

"Different?" Mom repeated, glancing about the room as if she could find the source of my discontent and eradicate it as she would a virus.

"It's softer," I said, joining her at the window and looking out at the open fields. "Greener."

"All those trees, Millie," Dad said, patting at my back. "Look at all those pines."

"They're pretty," I admitted.

And they were. But they didn't hold a candle to the magnolias currently bursting into bloom across my backyard right now.

My old backyard, I reminded myself.

"Coming, coming!" Dad shouted as a mover called up the stairwell. "Let's get through this day and we'll celebrate tonight, all right?" He kissed my mom's forehead before jogging downstairs.

"Celebrate?"

Mom nodded and ruffled my dark blond locks. They were long overdue for a trim. I'd planned on getting a haircut during spring break, but by then the salons were closed. Dad very helpfully volunteered to lop it all off with his clippers.

Um, thanks, no.

I'd taken to wearing it in a giant topknot instead.

"We made it here," she explained. "There were a lot of moments we didn't think it would happen. But we did. And that's worth celebrating, isn't it?"

"I suppose so." I ran my finger along the red curtains. They really were terrible.

I wanted to say more, but a burly mover stepped into the room, his arms impossibly laden down with boxes marked MILLIE.

"We'll think up something fun," she said. "I promise."

—

"I've never hurt so much in my entire life," I said hours later, collapsing onto the rug.

The movers had left and for the first time, it was just the three of us in the house. It was simultaneously too quiet yet alive with a host of unfamiliar sounds. The old wooden floorboards squeaked and something in the basement Dad called a sump pump kept issuing unexpected and startling thuds. We hadn't had a basement in our old house and the one here was full of spiderwebs and weird shadows.

It felt like that calm before the storm in any horror movie. The happy family moves into a new-to-them-but-still-very-old house, and things are good but night falls and then . . .

I paused, waiting for something weird to happen.

A box mysteriously toppling over.

A flock of birds flying into the window.

Blood seeping down the staircase.

Nothing stirred and I begrudgingly rolled over.

Mom lay sprawled across the couch, her feet propped on too many throw pillows. She was rubbing at her temples as if warding off a headache. Dad was on the floor beside me, trying to stretch out a kink in his back.

"What a day," he said, wincing as his spine cracked. "That's better. What are we doing for dinner, Molly?"

"There's nothing in the fridge," Mom said, opening her eyes. "We'll have to go grocery shopping tomorrow." She paused, self-correcting. "We'll have to place an order for groceries tomorrow."

"Think they'll deliver, all the way out here?"

"We'll see. Why don't we order in tonight?" She pulled out her phone, fiddling with it for a second before frowning. "I don't have any data, do you?"

None of us did.

Or reception.

This explained a lot.

My phone had been unnaturally quiet all day. I'd worried my friends in Memphis had already forgotten about me, but maybe there was a whole slew of messages waiting for me, they just couldn't deliver.

"Maybe a neighbor has open Wi-Fi?" I swiped hopefully through my settings.

"What neighbors?" Dad asked as the available networks list came up completely blank.

I stared at it uneasily. This was it. This was where all the scary movie stuff would start happening and there would be no way to call for help. "What . . . what do we do now?"

Mom pushed herself off the couch. "I think I saw an actual phone book someplace."

"What good will that do? There's no network."

Her laugh carried across the hall. "There's a landline in the kitchen."

I'd noticed the olive green phone on the wall when we'd first walked through the house. It was one of those old rotary ones with the round plate you swung in a circle to enter the numbers and a spiral cord that hung almost all the way to the floor.

"Does it actually work?" I asked, trailing after her curiously.

Mom laughed again, her amusement tinkling through the house and almost making it feel like home. She pulled a surprisingly slim yellow pages from a cabinet drawer and blew off a layer of dust.

"Mom, that thing has to be a decade old."

She flipped through the sections, undeterred.

"Looks like our choices are pizza or . . . pizza."

"Pizza it is," I said, leaning against her shoulder to read the ads.

"Which sounds better—Big Mike's Pizza Haven or Slice of Bliss?"

"Bliss me, baby," Dad voted, groaning as he flipped over. "I feel like Big Mike has already done a number on me today."

Mom reached for the phone before pausing and pulling out her trusty roll of disinfecting wipes. She'd been carrying them around the house all day, wiping down handles and cabinet doors. She cleaned off the handset, then began dialing. I liked the clicking stutter of the numbers rolling back.

"Hi, we're new to the area and wondered if you deliver

out to the west side of town . . . we're on Milner Avenue?" She recited the address and listened for a long moment to his response. "Perfect! We'd like to order a large pepperoni and mushroom. And—we weren't able to check online—do you have any salads? . . . Great! The Garden Melody, family-sized."

From the living room, Dad groaned. I curled the cord around one finger, watching as my skin turned purple, then white.

"And garlic knots, if you have them."

He cheered.

"Better make that a double order," she said, rolling her eyes at me with a grin.

"Okay . . . yes . . . Cash. That's perfect. . . . Thanks! We'll see you soon." She hung up the phone with a victorious click. "Here in thirty. Apparently they're not far. Just down Davis Way," she said, joining Dad on the floor. "Oh. This was a mistake. Throw me a pillow, Millie? Or twelve?"

I tossed a pair at her.

"So . . ." I waited till she and Dad were situated comfortably, listening to the seconds tick by, marked by the grandfather clock in the hall. "Tomorrow . . . Big day."

They were both due at the hospital lab at nine on the dot, leaving me here to start making headway on all of the house stuff. It had sounded terribly impressive at first—I would be the one deciding where everything went, creating order from the chaos.

Now, looking around, it just felt like a lot of work.

"Big day," Dad agreed. "Look, Mills—I know it feels like we're leaving you in the lurch . . ."

I scanned the wall of boxes waiting to be unpacked. "It *is* a little overwhelming."

"And it's so not how we wanted this to happen," Mom said, rushing in. "This outbreak has just . . . derailed a lot of stuff. We're so, so fortunate to have this set of problems and not others," she added quickly. "But I do want to fully acknowledge this is not ideal for you. But . . . we're going to be home all weekend to help. We're certainly not expecting you to do this all yourself."

"But if we came home tomorrow night to a totally straightened house and a gourmet meal . . ." Dad waggled his eyebrows at me.

Mom swatted at him with one of the pillows. "Steve!"

I picked at the label on the nearest box. LIVING ROOM—BOOKS. "It'll be fine. I'll just . . . choose a room and start opening stuff, right?"

"I'd go with the kitchen," Dad recommended.

"Yeah, about that. We don't have any food," I pointed out.

"We'll order groceries," Mom promised. "I'll do it on my lunch break at the lab. And the cable company is supposed to be out here tomorrow, so we'll be up and running soon."

"And that's . . . safe?" I asked, an uncomfortable knot lodging beneath my sternum. I didn't want to admit how much the idea of germs now scared me. Particularly to my parents, who were around them daily. "I mean, I thought the whole reason

Aunt Carla couldn't come help us was because we're supposed to be social distancing, or whatever."

"That's true, but Carla is staying away more for her protection than ours."

Mom's sister had lupus, which could make it harder to fight COVID if she was infected. Corona. I still wasn't sure what term I was supposed to be using. No one else seemed to either.

"And the cable company assured me they're taking every precaution. Masks, gloves, the works."

"They have masks?"

There'd been reports of shortages.

Mom shrugged. "Wear yours, just to be safe."

We fell into silence, each thinking of the day to come. The gears of the grandfather clock wound up to count out the quarter hour. The sump pump thunked again.

The doorbell rang.

"That was fast." Dad started to hoist himself up but crashed back. "Nope. Not happening."

"Mill, can you get it? There're a couple of twenties in my wallet," Mom said, rubbing at her hip.

It wasn't until I stomped to the front of the house that I realized how dark it had gotten. Guiltily, I flicked the outdoor lights on, illuminating an empty porch. Opening the door, I peered out into the dusky twilight.

Spring peepers sang their little frog songs, and I was certain it was the prelude for a machete-waving maniac to come striding around the corner.

"Hey there," a voice called out from the yard.

I tensed, then immediately shook it off. Neither Jason nor Michael Myers were known for their chatty banter.

I really was going to have to stop it with the scary movies living out here.

"Sorry we didn't have the light on," I said, squinting. A form came out of the darkness. "Oh."

The guy's mask covered his face from the bridge of his nose down to his chin. It was homemade, with a floral print, probably created from the remnants of a fabric scrap bin. He was tall and lanky and looked about my age—as far as I could tell.

"Didn't want to startle you," he said, gesturing to the mask with his shoulder. His hands were full of boxes and the bag of salad was looped around his forearm.

"I like the flowers."

He laughed. "My mom made it for me. I begged her to get some cooler fabric. They've got to make something with the Pistons logo, right?"

"You like basketball?" I asked, instantly warming.

"Yeah. It sucks they put the season on hold. I mean . . . there was no way we were going to make the playoffs this year, but still . . ."

"We were," I defended quickly. "The Grizzlies, I mean. I'm from Memphis. Was." A flush of red flared across my face. "We just moved here."

"Yeah, I saw the sign in the yard. Do you play?"

I nodded.

I can't be entirely sure, but I think he smiled. His eyes narrowed into little crescent moons, framed by impossibly thick

11

sooty lashes. "Cool. Me too. Maybe we can do a pickup game sometime. When all this is over. I'm Luka," he added.

"Millie."

His eyes curved at the corners—he was smiling again, maybe. "I guess I should probably give you your food now, before it gets cold."

"Right. Here," I said, thrusting the money out at him before quickly dropping my hand, horrified at how easy it was to forget I wasn't supposed to go near him. "How do we do this?"

He laughed. "It's totally weird, right? I've been leaving stuff on the porch at other people's houses. You set the money there and then we'll do a whole *Bridge of Spies* trade-off."

"Okay." I put the twenties on the porch, then stepped back with a slow theatricality that made him laugh again. It was such a happy sound, I wanted to hear it again and again.

He came forward and set the boxes down, leaving the bag on top. Quick as a wink, he snatched the money, counting it out. Now in the glow of the porch light, I noticed the waves of his dark hair were more than a little shaggy, definitely due for a trim.

"Need change?"

"Nope, all yours." His eyes lit up and I realized I must have given him an outrageous tip.

"Nice. Thanks! Well . . . welcome to the neighborhood, Millie. Have a good night."

"You too—stay safe."

He nodded, dipping back into the yard's darkness. With a final wave, he was gone.

—

I sliced the razor down the center of the packaging tape with unnecessary panache. After a morning of unpacking, I'd become an expert at popping the boxes open with just three flicks of the blade.

Give me a set of box cutters and I'd totally be a Final Girl in whatever slasher film you wanted to cast me in.

This was the last of the kitchen boxes. I swept my eyes over the space, proud of the work I'd accomplished. Plates, bowls, and cups were stacked behind the glass display cabinets with organized clarity and the lower drawers were full of pots and pans. Cheery red towels hung off the oven and dishwasher racks, adding a pop of color against all the oak. I'd even put up our collection of magnets on the fridge, adding the Slice of Bliss one Luka had included in the salad bag last night.

Remembering the pizza made my stomach growl with a sudden ferocity. After I sorted through this final box of silverware, I'd take a break and dive into the leftovers.

But before I could start, the doorbell rang, chiming loudly in the quiet of the house.

"Finally!" I exclaimed, making my way to the front.

My phone held far more photos than it did music or podcasts and with Dad's old radio still packed away somewhere, the morning had been brutally quiet. I'd forlornly imagined all the Zoom meet-ups my friends were holding without me. Last week Zoe had mentioned wanting to DIY her own highlights and we'd all gleefully promised to watch her livestream the disaster.

I slipped a mask over my face, wincing as one of the elastic straps twisted into my flyaways, yanking at the strands of hair, then opened the door.

A man in gray coveralls stood just off the porch, a good six feet away. He had on a blue mask and white latex gloves.

"Hi, hi, come in!" I greeted him, stepping back to allow him access through the door.

He hung back, his thick eyebrows furrowing into a solid line of confusion. "Miss?"

"You're with the cable company, right? To install the Wi-Fi?"

He nodded. "I already got you all set up outside—checked all the lines and you should be good to go."

I tilted my head. "But don't we need a . . . box . . . or a router, or whatever?"

"They're all in there. HDMI cables and the remotes too." He pointed to a bag on the porch I'd just noticed.

"Okay . . ." I trailed off, still not following. "Want me to bring it in for you?"

"I can't come inside the house, miss," he said. "Company policy. The rep should have told you?"

They might have told Dad all that when he'd set up the appointment, but he'd certainly not passed it along to me.

I blinked hard. My eyes felt itchy from all the dust I'd kicked up while cleaning.

"So . . . what am I supposed to do?"

"Everything you need is in there," he said, pointing to the bag again. "Instructions too."

"*I'm* supposed to set it up?" I asked, realization dawning on me. I sneezed once.

"Or your parents," he suggested. "Your dad. If he's not too sick."

Ignoring the implied sexism, I stepped onto the porch to rummage through the bag. As I came forward, he faltered back, keeping his distance.

"I'm not sick. It's just allergies." I pulled out a mess of cables. "I don't . . . How am I supposed to—"

"The instructions are in there," he repeated, shifting his weight from foot to foot. "If you've got questions, there's a number to call."

I flashed unhappily back to the rotary phone.

"You're sure you can't just come in and set it up?" I tried, smiling my widest grin before realizing he couldn't see it. "We just moved here, and nothing works right now. I swear, none of us are sick."

Of course, I sneezed again. Final Girl indeed.

"It's just all the dust, from the boxes and everything."

Another sneeze.

He shook his head adamantly. "It's against company policy."

"Okay, but—"

"Just call the number if you have any questions," the technician said, inching closer to his van. "Oh, and when you do, make sure to tell them you were satisfied with our visit today.

15

Those surveys really help with our numbers. Anything less than a ten is a failure for us!"

He was halfway down the drive before I could even think to laugh at the utter absurdity.

—

"He wouldn't come inside?" Mom repeated an hour later over the phone. She'd called the landline and so I'd perched on the kitchen cabinet to talk, twirling the spiral cord around my fingers in an unconscious gesture, over and over.

"And I went through everything in the bag but I still don't know how to set it up. He said I could call if I had questions but the phone cord doesn't reach the cable outlet."

I felt like I was in one of those inane comedy shows where someone was about to pop out from behind a couch, pointing a camera while cackling at my surprise.

"We'll get it figured out when we get home," she promised. There was a pause. "We'll be a bit late tonight."

"Why?" My mind instantly jumped to the worst-case scenario.

They'd already started working with the virus.

There'd been an accident.

Dad was infected.

He was already intubated.

He was already—

"There's just a lot of stuff going on here—first days are always the worst, so tomorrow should be better, right?" Mom said, her voice brightening. She always tried grabbing onto any silver lining in reach.

"Is Dad okay?" I hated how small my voice sounded. He, my mother, any and all of us were only one wrong breath away from the end. It was scarier than anything Guillermo del Toro could ever conjure up.

"Of course. He's fine. It's . . . a lot of to take in, but he's fine."

"And you?" I pressed.

"Both of us are fine, I swear, Millie."

"You'd tell me if . . ." I didn't want to finish the sentence but Mom knew what I meant. I could picture a smile softening her face.

"You know I would. That said," she drew out, changing tones. "I do have a little bit more bad news. I got the groceries ordered and scheduled for delivery, but they won't come till Thursday."

It was Tuesday now.

"And I'm guessing you ate the leftovers for lunch?"

"Yeah . . . I could drive into town," I offered. "Maybe pick up something."

"We took separate cars today," she said, nixing the idea. I glanced out the window, only now noticing the empty driveway. "In case our shifts ended at different times."

"I don't have money anyway," I said, remembering my wallet. It was tucked away in my dresser drawer. I hadn't touched it in weeks. What good was cash and a driver's license when you couldn't leave the house?

"Uh . . ." Mom went quiet for a moment, thinking through

options. "Looks like delivery again. I'll call that place we ordered from last night and see if they'll hold my card till you order. Whatever you want tonight. Go crazy, kid." Guilt colored her voice.

"Should I get something for you guys? I don't mind waiting till you're home to eat."

My stomach grumbled in protest.

"That's sweet, but I don't know when that'll be . . . The cafeteria here stays open till seven—or we'll get drive-through if it's late. The world may be ending, but there's always McDonald's, right?" She laughed but it wasn't as bright as before.

"Right." I bit my lip, wanting to say more, but felt emptied of words.

"I should get going. My break is almost over. I'll call the pizza place right now, though, okay?"

I nodded. "Thanks. Love you, Mom."

"Love you, Mills."

"I hope the rest of your shift goes—" The connection cut off before I could finish, and I set the heavy receiver back into its cradle with a click.

The sob escaped me as a swell of tears wet my eyes.

This sucked.

All of it.

The cable guy, too scared to come inside.

The groceries that wouldn't come till Thursday.

The silent, empty house. Mom and Dad should have been here. We should have all been piled around the dining room table, eager to hear about Mom's first day, Dad eager to talk about whatever he'd written for his book. I'd be eager about . . . something.

Maybe I'd have already met some people in the neighborhood.

Maybe I'd already have made a friend.

One whose face I could see.

But no.

I spotted my face mask on the counter and balled it in my hands, wanting to wring it out of existence.

This stupid, stupid virus. It was ruining everything.

The sound of ripped stitches stopped me cold. I'd torn off one of the elastic ear bands and its sad frayed edge sobered me up.

There were people all over the country, all over the *world,* who needed masks and I'd just destroyed one in a fit of petulant self-pity.

What kind of monster would do such a thing?

"A monster trapped in a house that's not her home and can't do anything for herself," I muttered, slumping to the kitchen floor, spent. I leaned against a cabinet front, bumping my head on its trim with a deep sigh.

Mom said the cafeteria was open till seven. That meant she might conceivably still be at the hospital at seven, sitting down for dinner, so she'd finish her shift . . . when?

I glanced at the clock on the stove. It was five-thirty now. Lunch seemed like days ago. I was crabby, tiptoeing on the edge of hangry.

I needed food.

Things always looked better when there was pizza.

Shoving off the floor, I swiped the Slice of Bliss magnet from the fridge, then turned to the rotary phone with trepidation.

I'd answered calls from my parents on it throughout the day, but I hadn't actually made a call myself. Poking my finger into the first numbered hole, I swiped the circle around, like I'd watched Mom do last night.

"Why are there so many zeros?" I muttered, waiting for the dial to swing back to its starting position. The last number finally clicked over.

"Slice of Bliss," an older woman answered after two rings. In the background, I could hear the cheerful commotion of their kitchen and an acute flare of envy stabbed me. I really did need to find Dad's radio.

"Hi . . . um . . . this is Millie Woodruff. My mom was supposed to call you guys to hold a credit card?"

"Just got off the phone with her, hon. What can I get you?"

"Um . . . a small pepperoni pizza . . . with extra green peppers. Wait, medium," I clarified, remembering I was also ordering tomorrow's meals. "And a thing of garlic knots."

I could hear the scratch of her pencil as she wrote it all down. "Okay. Should be there in about . . . forty minutes."

"Thanks. Do you know . . ." I started, then trailed off as my face flushed red.

"Do I know?"

I tucked a piece of hair behind my ear. "Do you know who will be delivering it? Um. You know, for safety . . . stuff."

There was a bark of laughter. "Luka will be there in forty."

The call clicked off and a moment later, the unfamiliar and wholly annoying drone of the dial tone filled my ear. I went back to unpacking, a smile on my lips.

—

Forty-two minutes later, a beat-up silver station wagon pulled up to the house and the same delivery guy hopped out.

Luka.

He had on another floral mask—red tulips this time—and it set off the blue of his eyes. Luka waved as he caught sight of me sitting on the porch steps, his arms impossibly long. Basketball player arms. My heart skipped a proverbial beat.

Gosh, he was gorgeous.

Probably.

But it was silly to ponder the mysteries beneath the mask. There was no way a guy like Luka didn't already have a girl-friend.

Probably a cheerleader, and they'd kiss at center court after his games and everyone would pretend to be grossed out but you couldn't truly hate on them because they were just too cute together.

Yup. Totally silly.

"Were you timing me?" He checked his watch before grab-bing the boxes from the passenger seat and shutting the door.

"Depends. Is there free pizza for me if you're late?"

His eyes crinkled with an unseen smile and he shook his

head. "Dad would have lost so much money when Kenny was delivering. Older brother," he explained.

I jumped to my feet, then felt awkward standing so many steps above him as he lingered in the yard, six feet away. Even with all my added false inches, we were eye to eye. "It's your family's restaurant?"

He nodded. "My grandpa started it. Bliss was my grand-mother's name. My parents took it over when Pops wanted to retire."

"And you and your brother work there now."

"Brothers," he corrected. "There are five of us. But I'm the only one still slinging pizza. Baby of the family."

His voice was light and wry and I found myself wishing I could see the smile that must be hiding beneath his mask, certain it would be as dazzling as he was.

"What about you? Do you have any brothers or sisters?"

"Only child."

"I can't imagine how peaceful your house must be!"

"Believe me, I think you've got it better. It was too peaceful here today."

He tilted his head, studying me. "Oh yeah?"

"Yeah . . . my parents both started work and it's just . . . weird being in a new house all day by yourself, you know?"

"I don't think I've *ever* been home by myself," he said with a laugh. "But at least you had total control over the remote, right?"

"There's no cable!"

His eyes widened. "What? No!"

22

I launched into my tale of woe. Luka was a good listener, nodding with interest, and I was pleased when he chuckled in all the right spots. My feet itched to step in closer, shrinking the wide gap between us, but my mind replayed the ads that had flooded the news, matches jumping out of place before they caught fire, contaminated surfaces glowing red and spreading, peaked curves sharp as a coffin.

I stayed put.

"Aw, that's terrible! I can't believe he just left the stuff on the steps." He glanced down at the boxes in his hands, recognition furrowing his eyebrows. "Well . . . maybe I can. There're so many new rules about everything, it's hard keeping track of what you're supposed to do. Like hand washing!"

My eyebrows raised in horror. "You didn't wash your hands before all this?"

He doubled over, snorting. "That's not what I meant! But like—I don't think I ever thought about how long I was supposed to wash them for. I just rinsed the soap off and went on my merry way."

"Not me. I always counted to twenty seconds. Twenty-five, actually."

"Liar. What song do you sing?"

"Song?" I repeated.

"You're supposed to sing 'Happy Birthday' to yourself twice."

"What's wrong with that?"

"You can't sing 'Happy Birthday' when it's not your birthday. Plus I was always craving cake."

"Cake does sound really good right now," I admitted.

"You should have ordered some."

I gasped theatrically. "Wait, you sell cake?"

"Oh yeah, it's what we're known for. Mom uses my grandmother's old recipes."

"What kind?"

He shrugged. "All kinds. What's your favorite?"

"Depends on what I'm in the mood for. Today I think my favorite is . . ." I paused thoughtfully. "German chocolate."

His eyes lit up. "Ooh, with the coconut and the pecans? Yeah, I could definitely go for that." He tsked. "Should have ordered some."

"I didn't know! You really ought to include something about cake in the phone book."

"Who uses the phone book?" He reached into his back pocket. "There you go, Millie Woodruff," he said, smacking a menu onto the pizza box and leaving everything on the porch. "Prepare to have your mind blown."

I picked up the trifold and scanned the dessert section, impressed. "These sound amazing."

"They are. . . . Hey, are you at Central?" He pointed to the paperback copy of *The Catcher in the Rye* I'd left open on the steps. "Mrs. Holwerda's English?"

I brightened. "I will be. In the fall. With all of the remote-learning stuff, my teachers are letting me finish the year in Memphis, even up here. Well . . . if I ever get the internet back."

It *had* been rather nice to not have eleven thousand emails and notifications chiming at me as assignments piled in.

"We're reading *Catcher* right now too. It just drags. And there's like no point to it, right?"

"You sound like such a phony," I teased.

"Why are they making us read it? Did you know that every serial killer ever has a copy of that book on them when they're caught?"

"Every serial killer?" I raised a dubious eyebrow.

"Look it up! Well, not right now, but later. The guy that killed the guy from the Beatles. JFK. Reagan." He counted his list on his fingers. "There are loads more."

"Reagan didn't die," I pointed out. "I mean, he's dead now, but it wasn't an assassination."

"All I'm saying . . . it's a seriously questionable book and we shouldn't be forced to read it."

"What *should* we be reading, then?"

He tilted his head, considering, and I tried not to notice the curve of his jawline. The mask accentuated it, clearly defining its angles, and I longed to rip it aside to admire the boy underneath.

"Something by Shirley Jackson, maybe."

I blinked, taken aback. Basketball, cake, and now spooky books?

Luka *was* the perfect guy.

And I had no idea what he—or his sure-to-be-impossibly-adorable-cheerleader-girlfriend—really looked like.

"I love her! I read *Hill House* last year when the show came out."

His eyes sparkled. "We *all* read *Hill House* last year when the show came out. I'm so excited for season two. Have you read *Turn of the Screw?*"

"Not yet."

"It's *so* good. One of my favorites. I've read it about fifty times. Old horror is so much better than the new stuff. I like when you have to really imagine all the creepy bits, not just have them come running out and smack you over the head. Like in—" He paused. "Sorry. I get really excited about books."

"Don't apologize! I love scary movies."

"Yeah? You'll go nuts over Henry James, then!"

"I'll look it up the next time I'm at . . ." I trailed off, a wedge of emotions lodged in my throat. I didn't know what the local bookstore here was and even if I did, it didn't matter. I wouldn't be able to go inside and mindlessly browse, looking up books that a cute guy recommended.

"Right . . ." Luka nodded with understanding. "Curbside delivery is all well and good but it's definitely not the same." His eyes flickered down to the Salinger. "We've got a test on that Friday."

"Us too!"

"That's funny. I could come over later if you want talk through—"

A tinny version of Weezer's "Africa" started playing, leaving my hopes hung impossibly high, pinned at the back of my

26

throat. I felt like I was at an amusement park, on the free-fall drop, the split second before gravity took over.

Come over.

He'd said he wanted to come over.

Here. To see me.

No pizza required.

"Err . . . hang on. . . ." He fished out his cell. "Hey. Yeah, I'm still over at—okay . . . Yeah, no worries . . . Okay. Okay, okay, okay. Love you too."

Love you too.

My heart sank. It was official. There was a girlfriend.

He lowered the phone, turning back to me. His mask puffed out as he released a deep sigh. "Sorry about that. Gotta run. Duty calls."

"Oh sure," I said, fumbling to think of a normal way to end the conversation. "Your girlfriend could come too—to study, if you want."

Great, Mills, totally normal.

His eyebrows quirked, head tilting in confusion. "Girlfriend? Oh, no—gosh no! That was my dad. Big emergency at the store. Some morons are throwing a 'social distancing party'"—he turned his fingers into air quotes, rolling his eyes—"and ordered like thirty pizzas."

"Oh geez. That's not . . . that's not good at all."

"Nope," he agreed. "But he really needs another set of hands. I should get going." He jogged back to his car. "Later, Millie."

"Later, Luka," I echoed, scooping up the boxes and offering a wave as the station wagon roared to life.

He started backing out of the driveway, then stopped, rolling down his window. "Just so you know—there's no girlfriend in the picture. Like, at all."

"Oh. Well. That's good," I stammered, mortified to have been so thoroughly seen through.

"I just thought I should make that clear."

My cheeks flushed with a delicious heat as he took off his mask, tossing it into the passenger seat. His grin was easy and wide and I'm sure it was dazzling, but really the only thing I noticed was the gleam in his eyes as he winked at me.

Before I could respond, he was at the end of the drive, giving his horn a friendly beep. I stood on the porch long after the red of his taillights disappeared, feeling happier than I had in days.

—

"Morning, Mills," Dad greeted me as I stumbled into the kitchen.

"You're up early."

I'd fallen asleep long before they'd come home, passed out on the couch in an exhausted stupor after getting half the living room boxes unpacked. Someone, probably Mom, had tucked a quilt around me.

"Lots to do." He was already dressed for work, perched on a stool, eating a slice of cold pizza straight out of the box.

"That was my lunch!" I protested.

He studied the crust with a wry grin. "No . . . Pretty sure that was my breakfast. Good call on the extra peppers."

"Dad! The groceries don't come till tomorrow."

"You'll be fine. There're two slices left, plus that bag of whatever."

I grabbed a glass from the shelves and crossed to the sink. "What bag?"

"There was a bag on the porch last night when we got in. Had the pizza logo on it. I stuck it in the fridge for you."

I blinked, frowning at the box he was eating out of. "But I brought the pizza in."

He shrugged, closing it. "I gotta get going. Mom already left. She told me to tell you she got the router figured out. Internet is up and running."

"She did? When?"

Dad laughed. "Your guess is as good as mine. The woman never sleeps." Glancing at the clock on the coffeemaker, he wrinkled his nose. "I'm going to be late." He ruffled my hair before planting a kiss on my forehead. "Kitchen looks good, Millie. I'm impressed. Keep it up."

"Have a good day at work," I said, trailing after him to the front door. "Hope it's not another long one."

He made a face. "Think there are going to be a lot of those for the time being. Chin up, though." Dad let out a little half-laugh-half-groan. "There are signs with that all over the hospital. 'Chin up. Masks on.' It's bled into my subconscious."

"Sounds like the new 'Keep Calm and Carry On.'"

"We should make greeting cards. Get on that, okay?" A quick hug and he was off.

I stood at the window, watching him leave and listening to the soft sounds of the empty house.

Another day on my own.

But at least there would be music.

Maybe Weezer, I thought with a smile.

My laptop was still in the living room. The TV was useless without streaming, so I'd fallen asleep watching an old Hitchcock film, one of the few DVDs I'd hung on to in the move. Battery totally drained, I took it into the kitchen to charge.

As the computer hummed back to life, I spotted the pizza box still on the counter. In his race out the door, Dad had forgotten it. I was tempted to dive into the last slices for breakfast but then remembered the bag Dad had mentioned.

Curiosity sent me to the fridge, where a Slice of Bliss bag sat innocuously in the middle of the empty shelves. I shoved the pizza back into the cold confines and took out the bag, utterly bemused as I peered inside.

It was a book.

A book on a box.

I traced my fingers across its cracked spine. "Henry James," I read aloud. A flutter of delight sparked within me and I knew I wouldn't be getting many boxes opened today.

Flipping through the tattered pages, I saw dozens of underlined sentences and notes scribbled in the margins. It looked just like my favorite books. Well loved and thoroughly beat to hell.

I set the book aside and turned to the box. A thick slice of German chocolate cake, dark and drizzling, peered up at me. On the inside flap of the box, a note was scrawled in thick slanted lines.

You won't find this in any textbook, but I have it on good authority Salinger once said that chocolate cake was Holden's favorite. I'm off Wednesday—want to hang out? Six feet apart, of course. Luka.

With a ridiculous grin plastered across my face, I picked up the telephone and dialed the numbers, fingers dancing over the rotary with impatience.

"Hi, I'd like to place an order . . . Chocolate cake . . . two slices . . . For delivery."

The Socially Distant Dog-Walking Brigade

by Bill Konigsberg

The first time I met Daxton O'Brien, my dog Griffin peed on him.

I was out walking Griffin and we were in the park near my house, across from the weird alcove with the community garden and the small rock sculptures. The neighborhood has made it into an unofficial dog park, where it's okay to let your dog off leash. It's my favorite place in the world, because dogs. Way, way better than people. Low bar.

I always try to get Griffin to run there, but he's not a dog that really understands play. I take him off leash and he just sits at my side, hoping for liver treats. Cut to him an hour later, staring at me with his mouth open and panting while I'm bingeing *Top Chef* on the couch. I'm like, *You had your chance, buddy.*

We were alone in the small, shaded, grassy square when a

mini-parade of dogs marched by. I don't mean like the dogs were on floats dancing, or there was a marching band and confetti; there were just six dogs.

They were all attached by leashes to people, yes, but who sees people when you can look at dogs?

In front was a gray Siberian husky, prancing like it owned the sidewalk. Then came a pair of Chihuahuas, yipping up a storm, one white and one black. Following them was a caramel-colored Pomeranian that looked like it was wearing a large-collared fur coat. Then a Weimaraner, all smooth and gray. And in the rear, an overenthusiastic doodle of some sort that was trying to sniff seven things at once. It looked a lot like my Griffin, only with black fur instead of apricot.

The Pomeranian's person, a middle-aged lady I'd seen before, wearing red librarian glasses, waved toward me. I waved back, hoping she'd keep walking. Nothing to see here. I just wanted Griffin to do his business so I could go home and actively avoid distance-learning by playing Design Home on my phone. Griffin is sort of indifferent to other dogs, sort of like me with people.

I scanned them quickly. They were masked and appropriately distanced, and it reminded me of the one good thing about this pandemic: having a reason to steer clear of people. It can be hard to tell with masks, but the first four were clearly adults, and the one in back looked like a teenager, just about my age. One of their kids, maybe? He was skinny with blond hair and a long, thin face, and he was attempting to rodeo-wrangle the overenthusiastic doodle.

The guy in the front stopped and cupped his hands over his mask, and warily I put my hand to my ear. He lowered his mask to his chin, entirely negating the purpose of the mask in the first place. He had a bushy salt-and-pepper mustache.

"Your dog safe?" he yelled.

Safe? Like from the coronavirus? I was confused. I cupped my mask-covered mouth and yelled "What?"

"Does your dog play well with others?"

"Oh, um. Yeah, I guess. He's . . . safe."

I got that churning in my stomach that comes with the proximity of people. Maybe it's my body's reaction to danger. Fight or flight, I guess they call it. I tried to slow my breathing as the bunch of them strolled over until they were about ten feet away. They simultaneously unleashed their dogs, and Griffin went charging up to each of them to say hello. He sniffed the teen boy's dog's butt. He did that weird circle dance with the Pomeranian, where both dogs tried to get to the other's behind.

It's always weird, that moment where your dog starts sniffing another dog's butt, and you're standing there with their human, and suddenly you're uncomfortably aware of both of your butts, and it's like, *Hi there, other person with a butt!* Fortunately, the older guy's husky reared back in that *let's play* position, and Griffin took off across the park.

When he's in the mood, the boy loves to be chased.

I avoided conversation by turning my head to watch. As they ran in a large circle at the perimeter of the park, Griffin looked like a big pile of apricot-colored fur blowing in the wind.

"Your dog is adorable," the woman said.

"Um, yours too," I said, having no idea where her Pomeranian even was at the moment.

And then it was quiet, which is the worst. Silence can be so awkward, but talking to strangers has never been in my skill set.

So the silence stayed, and it was Satan incarnate. Sometimes when I'd go to a party and wind up small-talking with someone, and they'd be droning on about how it was so hot in the summer—duh—or they hated doing homework, or something similarly banal, I would tune out, watch their facial muscles expand and contract, and I'd wonder what would happen if I just opened my mouth and started screaming.

Probably not get invited back. Which would be okay, I guess.

I glanced over at the guy my age, who was taller and better built than me. I looked away, afraid he'd see me looking. He was clearly a "Normal." It was obvious, from his red board shorts and yellow tank top and sandals, that he was one of those people who effortlessly fit in.

Normals are tricky. They had made my life a living hell, for two years, ever since eighth grade. You had to be careful around Normals, because sometimes they shape-shifted, like with Nimo back in February. My first. We were hanging out, and they drew me in by revealing their own supposed not-normalness. And then you let your guard down, and I guess maybe they get tired of whatever they were doing with you, and now they know all your darkest, most painful stuff. And they revert back to Normal without telling you, and they never talk to you again, and take your two best friends with them.

Yes, you had to be very careful around Normals.

Griffin came running back over, a wide grin across his face, panting. He trotted up to the boy all friendly, turned ninety degrees, lifted up his leg, and he peed.

"Wha!" was all I could say.

"Whoa," the boy finished for me, jumping back.

There was that split second before everyone started laughing where I actually thought: *Run! Just run, never look back, never see those people again.* But then they did laugh, and I was stuck, and all the attention was on me, and I hated my life so hard.

"Oh my god. I'm so sorry. Um."

Everyone was laughing, including the boy, but I was dying inside. "I'm so, um. He's never, ever, ever done that before. Never ever ever. Sorry. Sorry. Sorry."

The boy shrugged, shaking his leg. The bottom of his red shorts and his leg seemed to take the hit. "I didn't like these shorts anyway."

"He owns you!" the older guy was yelling. "He peed on you, now he owns you!"

And I was like, *No, please stop talking.*

—

I avoided the park the next morning, for obvious reasons. Instead I headed down to Pinchot, which is pronounced Pin-Chot rather than Pin-Cho, because America. Pinchot is the best street in all of Phoenix for walking a dog. Back in the day it was part of the New Deal. They subdivided land into one-acre properties and encouraged industrial workers to farm part time. Apparently, Eleanor Roosevelt planted some trees on it. That was like the 1930s version of Beyoncé planting trees today, so it was kind of a big deal. And now, nearly a hundred years later, there's this incredible canopy of eighty-foot-tall Aleppo pines and Washington palms on Pinchot between 26th and 27th Streets. The whole street smells like pine and fresh-cut grass.

We lived a block north, where things smelled decidedly less lovely and trees were sparse and mostly small palms. Which was why I always walked on Pinchot.

And as if the world were punking me, there they were, the same dog-walking brigade, or at least three of them, heading toward me. The woman and the man were up front and about five feet apart, and when I craned my head, I saw Griffin's pee victim and his black doodle.

I thought about running, and this time I almost did, but then the woman waved to me again, and I sighed and realized running away would make it worse. So I kept walking, like a man toward his executioners. And while I walked, I thought about funny things I could say about the fact that yesterday Griffin had used the boy like a fence post. I came up with, *I've stopped allowing Griffin to drink water, so you should be safe.*

But when I approached them and opened my mouth, it burst out as "Drinking water, I've stopped . . . ," which didn't make any sense at all.

"Hydration is important," the woman with the librarian glasses said, nodding, as if what I'd said was somehow a normal greeting to near strangers. I thought about fixing it, but the moment was gone, so instead I just stood there and held Griffin's leash tightly, lest he do it again. Maybe the kid was some sort of pee magnet? Who was to say?

Then Griffin did one of his Griffin things. Out of nowhere he barked, turned his head both ways, and, as if he were suddenly sure he was being stalked by a zombie, he jumped a full one-eighty, his head leading the way. And then he jumped back, and just as quickly, he returned to normal, as if whatever had just possessed him had flown away. It used to scare me when Griffin acted nuts. Now I just understood it was Griffin being Griffin.

"What the heck?" the older guy said.

"Yeah," I mumbled, and a thing came to me as a coherent sentence, which was unusual but welcome in this case. "Griffin is basically that kid in school who sits in the back, eating chalk."

The boy laughed and when he did so, his eyes lit up. I couldn't see his mouth, but I imagined him with a smile where his lips pull up so high you can see his glistening gums.

This led to some laughter and the other people saying

various things, none of which I heard because I was playing back in my head the moment where I successfully said something funny, and in that way, maybe Normal, almost. And who was to say what Normal really was? And then I came to, and they were all looking at me, and I realized: Me. I was to say. And as previously noted, saying is not my strongest skill. Especially in front of a (potentially) good-looking boy (stupid masks). I am especially tongue-tied in the presence of (hypothetical) long-faced beauty.

So I opened my mouth, and my brain was suddenly extraordinarily empty, as if my one joke had cored me out, and the stupidest thing was that I knew as soon as I walked away, all the good things to say would come, because of course, the English language consists of many, many words, and they can be arranged in all sorts of order to make meaning. But there I was, standing like a statue, with my mouth open like an idiot, and it wasn't getting better, the longer I stayed that way.

So I said, "Bye."

And they each said, "Bye."

And I walked on, knowing for the entire month of May, and for however long this pandemic thing was going on, my only goal would be to never see those people again.

—

From that point on, I stayed on the west side of 26th Street, which was decidedly less beautiful, less canopied with huge trees, and therefore less shady, which definitely mattered in

Phoenix between May and September, when the flaming sun was only six or seven feet above the city at all times. Which was why I had to wake up at five-something every day to walk. Because walking dogs once the sidewalk had started to sizzle was evil and abusive, and I'd never ever do that to poor Griffin.

And maybe it was three days later, as I turned the corner from 25th Place onto Pinchot, that I saw, again, coming toward me like an unstoppable force, the masked brigade and their canines. And I thought, *God, why are you doing this to me? Isn't COVID-19 enough?*

But it wasn't, and as I walked toward them, Griffin pulling me forward the whole time, I had nothing. Nothing in my brain to say. So as I approached, I pasted on a smile they couldn't see beneath my mask, and I said, "Hi!" and kept walking, and they all said "Hi" back. Followed by the most surprising three words of the entire pandemic thus far.

The boy turned to me as I passed, motioned my way with his hand, and said, "Walk with us."

I turned and followed, like an obedient dog, all the while my heart pumping like I had just been threatened with a painful death rather than just walking with a bunch of strangers. I walked alongside the boy, behind the group of adults, my thump-thumping heart making it hard to hear and harder to breathe. The adults up ahead chatted with each other, and we two non-adults lagged behind.

He didn't say anything for a while, which actually kind of helped, because it made me feel like maybe he didn't think it was so weird that I wasn't saying anything. But as the silence stretched on, I thought maybe it was getting rude, so I gulped, decided to pretend I was someone who could conversate, and pointed to the teen boy's dog.

"Doodle?"

"Labra," he said.

"Me too. I mean, not me, mine. Is. Griffin," I said, and somehow I knew he knew I meant the dog. You never give out names with dog people, because who remembers people names?

"Squirrel," he said back.

I raised an eyebrow. "You named your dog Squirrel?"

Out of the corner of my eye I could see him lob his head around. He had shoulder-length hair the color of hay and tanned skin. His face was so thin it made me think of those vises in shop class, and I imagined his face in there getting squeezed, which was not nice or charitable but sometimes my brain goes to weird places. "My dad," he said. His voice from behind the mask was honeyed in that way that other queer kids sometimes talked, that way that made you kind of know it's okay, you're not going to get jumped. "He thought it would be funny at the dog park to yell 'Squirrel' when calling our dog, and all the other dogs would be like, 'Where's the squirrel?' Dad joke."

I grimaced and laughed despite myself. "Oh no he didn't."

"You know that thing where you think, like, *One good thing about the pandemic is I'll get to spend more time with my dad.* And then you do and you're like, *Yeah, no.*"

As we turned east on Earll, our dogs pulled toward the

church with the perfectly manicured green lawn Griffin enjoys writhing around on. We let them lead, and soon we had that weird moment when two dogs simultaneously squat, while you wait there, both holding an empty poop bag and avoiding eye contact.

And the guy, whose name I still didn't know, said, "Do dogs think we are mining them for their incredibly valuable poo?"

I was like, *What?*

He continued. "I mean, we house them, we feed them, we take them out, and when they poo, we collect it."

"Huh," I said. Wondering for the first time if maybe this kid was not so much a Normal.

"Daxton," he said.

"I thought you said Squirrel?"

"No, my name."

"Oh. Kaz," I said.

"Good to meetcha, Kaz. Meet us again tomorrow?"

Against my better instincts, I said yes. And I admit that I felt the slightest jolt of joy, imagining more conversations with the cute, queer boy who said not Normal things.

—

The next morning, after finding them on the corner of 27th and Earll, we paired off again, me and Daxton lingering back.

"Who are the adults?" I asked. "Are they your mom and dad?"

He laughed. "I wish. No. I just saw them walking one day

and I went up to them. They were really nice and invited me to walk with them, so I did."

I couldn't imagine doing that. But I could totally imagine Daxton doing it, and being totally normal about it.

"Cool," I said, meaning it.

Griffin pulled on the leash and I let up some, allowing him to peer around the oleander bush where, once a few years ago, he saw a small, brown feral cat. For the zillionth time in a row, it wasn't there, but I knew he'd expect to see it tomorrow. He's a very hopeful dog.

Then we walked some, six feet apart, both lost in our own thoughts.

"I think the pandemic is like God's way of telling humans to go to their room," he said, as we passed the house with the aqua and orange tile mosaics assembled on the mailbox and the concrete side wall.

I cracked up and pulled Griffin away from a bush of foxtail burrs. Those things were impossible to get out. This was not a very Normal thing to say, and I liked that. Still, shape-shifters. You had to be careful.

"And I don't mean like Pat Robertson's God, like someone trying to sell you something so your soul goes to the good place. More like actual God. Who is like a tree, or all trees, maybe. Who doesn't care if you're queer, like us."

I stopped walking. I'm basically out and everything, but. Adults. Not everyone is so okay with things. So I kinda meekly pointed ahead at them. They were walking maybe ten feet in front of us.

"They're adults in Central Phoenix. I'm pretty sure they know what queer teens look like."

We started walking again, and soon we found that we could hear each other from opposite sides of empty 27th Street, which was silent except for occasional dog barks and bird chirps. He was on the west side of the street, saving the east side and the rare shade from trees to me. The street was this cool hodgepodge of old farmhouses, some with untended desert landscapes, others showcasing English gardens in the middle of the desert. Behind shrubs and gates sat secret gardens that you could sometimes catch a glimpse of from the right angle. A few artists displayed mosaics that expressed gratitude, or joy, or peace, or Black Lives Matter. Praising health care workers. I loved it here.

"You out?" he called from the opposite side of the street.

I shrugged. I was, though perhaps not at the yelling-across-the-street level of outness. I was selectively out. At school with friends, yes. My mom knew, my grandma didn't. That sort of thing. No need poking the angry bear. Or, in this case, the Pentecostal bear who occasionally spoke in tongues.

"We moved here from Pinetop a few months ago," he said. "Great timing, right? I got like two months at my new school before it shut down. Me and my dad. It was so not okay up there."

That made sense to me. He'd been all closeted up for so long, and now that he could, he was wearing his queerness on his sleeve. Because he could. Griffin was veering left and right, like a prisoner on his one daily outing, which I suppose in a way he was. I stopped to let him sniff and then water a tall succulent that sat in front of a short peach fence. Daxton stopped too, and he crossed over toward where I was. I looked behind me, wanting to make sure there was enough room to give him distance.

"That makes sense," I said. "Do you like it here?"

He nodded. "I like my high school. School for the Arts, you know it?"

My eyes lit up. "Oh, cool."

"Yeah, my dad did okay on that one. He's like NASCAR Dad with a heart of gold. It's totally weird."

We lingered as our dogs sniffed near each other, and the two adults were far in the distance now. I pointed, as if to say we should hurry up, and he shook his head and said, "It's Caj."

I wasn't sure I should, because people don't like being corrected. But I took my chances.

I said, "Um. It's actually Kaz. Like with a *z*."

He gave me this look like, *What?*

Which was when it hit me that he meant their little dog-walking brigade. Was *caj*. As in short for *casual*. And I thought, *Why do I even speak, ever? This is why I should join a monastery.* So I nodded like I hadn't just made a fool of myself, and then I played the scene back in my head and realized that there was no way to avoid it, so I giggled. And he giggled. And that made the awkward feeling pressing against my chest go away.

"Hello, Kaz with a *z*," he said. "I'm Daxton with an *x*. And other letters."

I'm sure he could see I was blushing, but I hoped to god most of the red was under my mask.

We made a plan to meet up to walk the next day, and somehow, I didn't spend the entire day obsessing about conversation topics.

Who am I kidding? Of course I did.

—

The next day was one of those rare rainy days, when the sky sags in the corners, where it goes foreboding gray and you kind of know you might be in for a monsoon. We walked alone, just the two of us, and while I felt a little like Yoko Ono breaking up the Beatles, I liked it better this way.

He wore a black and red mask with the word *love* in cursive all over it. I wore a hospital-issue blue paper one. This seemed a little descriptive of the difference between me and Daxton.

What I longed to do was take my stupid mask off. Mostly because maybe it would get him to do the same and allow me to see Daxton's full face. Without seeing his mouth, it felt like I was still missing this essential part of who he was.

I pulled at my mask dramatically.

"Damn. I wish we could take these off."

"Tell me about it," he said. "But my dad has diabetes. He's high risk. I definitely can't."

I sighed, defeated. "Yeah. My mom works in a hospital. She'd kill me if she found out. On the plus side, at least I wouldn't die of the pandemic."

As we waved to the old lady with the German accent who sat on her porch in the mornings with her cats, Daxton said, "Do you ever get tired of yourself? Like, really tired?"

I stopped walking. Griffin pulled toward the cats, but my mind was on what Daxton had just said. I stared at him. Yes, of course I did. But this seemed like a trap. Like something a Normal says to make you let your guard down, and then they pummel you with it.

"I don't know."

He had stopped walking, too, as I guess he needed time and space to ponder my brilliant comment. Then he said, "Well. I sometimes think, like. I can never leave my brain. It's always talking, twenty-four-seven. I'm so sick of me."

And I thought, *Yes! Me too!* But I didn't dare say it. So instead, I nodded a lot as we strolled down different sides of Pinchot, and he shared things that were way too personal for me to ever say loud enough to be heard fifteen feet away, things about his mom's death, and his dad crying softly behind closed bedroom doors after. I watched him, wondering what it would feel like to be confident enough to share private stuff like that, and this little part of me wanted to say something about when my dad left two years ago, my mom told me we had thirty days to mourn, to cry and be sad, and then we had to be done. But I wasn't Daxton, and there was no way those words would ever breach my lips. So instead I nodded a lot, and said "yeah" and "right" a bunch of times, and when we got to my house, we paused, I did a meek little wave, and he wiped sweat off his forehead with the bottom of his tank top. Despite the cloudy day, it was already pretty hot. I tried not to stare at his bare belly button and the smooth musculature of his torso. It was weird. I had now seen that but not his mouth. I wondered if the first time I saw his actual mouth, it would be like the first time seeing Nimo naked.

"I'm sorry if the things I say make you uncomfortable," he said as his shirt sadly dropped back into position.

I swallowed. I shook my head fast.

"They don't?"

"No, I. Like the things. You say."

He gave me two thumbs up. "Okay. Cool."

Griffin pulled toward the front door, and I held tight because I had to say something. It was killing me to keep not saying everything.

So I said, "You are, out of your head, the way I am. In my head."

He cocked his head and raised an eyebrow. "What? I'm out of my head?"

"No. Ugh." I gathered myself. I breathed a few times. "The things you say. Out loud. They are like. The things I say, but only in my head."

The corners of his mask lifted, and he looked down at his feet, as if he were shy like me. He didn't say anything. Which was perfect because I didn't have any more, either.

—

48

Our walks became the focus of my days. They started getting longer, too, which was great for me and great for Daxton, and probably less great for Griffin and Squirrel, who, despite looking and acting alike, behaved like inmates at the same prison who were in different gangs.

"The thing about my dad is that he's selectively awful about my queerness," Daxton said one morning, a week later, as Griffin battled Squirrel for what appeared to be the optimal sniffing spot on my neighbor's white rock, the one I'd named "Urine Rock" because of Griffin's need to douse it first thing every morning.

"What do you mean?" I leaned against the old Goldwater pine on the edge of my neighbor's property.

"Ugh." He rolled his head all the way back. He was standing in the middle of the street. No cars because of the pandemic shutdown. "On the one hand, he's cool with it. He asks me if I have a boyfriend all the time like it's no big deal. And then there's 'the other team,' which I hate."

Squirrel attempted to mount Griffin, and he growled at her.

"What's 'the other team'?"

Daxton groaned. "When we watch a show or a movie, if he thinks someone might be gay, he'll nudge me. 'I think that guy's playing for the other team.' And I'm like, *Dad. What the hell team is this that you think we're on? I'm on the other team. You idiot.*"

"That sucks. What does he say when you say that?"

He kicked the asphalt below his feet and gently pulled

49

Squirrel toward him. Then he started to walk, so I followed. "Well, I only say it in my head. That may be one of the reasons he doesn't respond."

Our silences were comfortable by now. I didn't feel like I needed to fill up the emptiness with anything, and we just let them coast along with us as we strolled. I found myself walking at his side, maybe only four feet away, which wasn't far enough, probably, but it was like I couldn't bear to be far away from him. I glanced over to see his expression. He was looking down and there was this way his eyes appeared glassy in the midmorning sun that made me want to comfort Daxton, to reach out and touch him. He was right there, like if I stepped two steps toward him, those peach-fuzz-covered arms would be touchable. I realized it had been a really long time since Nimo. I longed to touch someone. But mostly, I longed to touch Daxton.

"I don't always speak up with my mom, either," I said.

He looked up, surprised, and it occurred to me I hadn't said much that was personal to Daxton in the time since we'd been walking. I wondered if maybe I shouldn't. If maybe this was too much, and I was opening up too much, like with Nimo. Like with Gus and Cyndi, my former friends who could now gargle Clorox for all I cared. Cross me once, shame on you. The end. I don't need this second-time stuff.

"It's like she's 'Busy Mom.' Not just now with the COVID thing, but that doesn't help. Always. And because she works and she's a mom, when she says something that isn't okay, I just feel like, *Well, that was close enough.* Like the time she said

Nimo would one day wake up and realize she's actually a girl, not a boy. I was like, *Whut?* But then I felt guilty, because she works so hard. I didn't say anything."

"Yes!" he shouted, his voice seemingly echoing in the silence of the morning. "It's like my dad could be so much worse, and he brought me down here into the city where it's safer for me, so I don't give him crap when he's kinda shitty. Like this one time this winter. I walked into the kitchen to get a soda, and he was on the phone with my uncle Arnie, who is awful, by the way, and I walked in just in time to hear him say, 'something something, if I had a real son.'"

I exhaled and gawked, thinking about how that must have made Daxton feel.

"So that happened. I don't even know if he saw me, because I just walked right out. And the rest of the day I was like, 'Look at me, Dad! I'm a real boy! Like Pinocchio or some shit.'"

My gut twisted. Poor Daxton. Who so didn't deserve that. Who was just this amazing, dynamic person, and his dad was negating like his entire existence. And suddenly I wanted to touch him even more, and I fucking hated COVID-19.

So after we watched Griffin scratch his ear manically with his left leg, and after I stared momentarily at Daxton's tanned legs, which were shapely but not overly muscular, like he ran cross-country but not track, I softly said some words that were probably going to end in my humiliation, but I honestly couldn't keep them in anymore.

"Well, I think you're a real boy. Very real."

I waited for the world to explode, because I was so cheesy

or whatever. Cheesy and awkward as fuck. But it didn't explode. We both kept walking, and I wanted to glance over but I thought if I did, and he was looking horrified, I might actually just die.

The quiet went a minute, and finally I realized I had to look over at him.

His eyes were focused on me, like shining. As if they were smiling. The mask didn't matter. I gulped.

"You are also a real boy, Kaz with a z," Daxton said. "Among other good things."

"Queer boys bringin' the realness," I said, because I'm stupid.

He laughed. "You listen, Kaz. And also, when you say stuff, it's good stuff. Like if I had to choose one person to be in quarantine, hands down it would be you, Kaz."

Chills, all over my body, even as the hot Phoenix sun blazed down on my back and shoulders.

"I would, also," I said. "Like to be with you. In quarantine."

And it was so awkwardly formal that we both laughed, and Squirrel picked this as the perfect time to try to mount Griffin again, and there was something so symbolic about it that we both left it unspoken.

—

The next morning, I awoke earlier than I even had to, and I showered, which I normally didn't do in the morning because it's not like anyone will get within sniffing distance anyway. And I paced the kitchen and then, when I couldn't wait

52

another second, I leashed up Griffin and went and sat on the concrete of my driveway.

It was just getting warm, and it heated up my legs nicely, and I thought about the things I was going to say today. To Daxton. Who liked the things I said. Who was trustworthy. I thought about telling Daxton about Nimo. It was hard to talk about Nimo, because of how it ended.

Basically, we went out for two months. And the whole time, they were like, 'What are you so afraid of?' because they were super open with me and told me all sorts of things. I was afraid, I guess. Because when you tell people stuff, it's like you uncross the arms you've had folded over your chest, and that's scary. But then, one day, we were having such a good time at this food truck festival at Salt River Fields, eating way more sugar than two people ever should, and I guess eating fry bread loosens some people up, because I just . . . uncrossed. I told Nimo everything: about my dad leaving, about how lonely it was at home sometimes, about cutting myself. They seemed to listen and they said all these supportive things, and I un-clenched my life, which I almost never do. I was beginning to think I was maybe in love with them.

But the problem with unfolding your arms is you leave yourself wide open.

The next day at school, Nimo was distant. Before school. Between classes. I finally cornered them in the cafeteria, and they were like, "I thought we were casual, but it's getting kinda intense. I need some space." And just like that, it was over. My friends Gus and Cyndi started hanging with Nimo, and that meant I had no one. And I spent a lot of time alone, thinking about how I would probably not be that open with anyone again. It hurts too much.

I sat there thinking a lot about Nimo, and also how it would be to actually tell Daxton, who would understand, because he seemed to get me. And Griffin got tired and lay down on his side on the concrete, which was now beginning to heat up.

That was when I realized: No Daxton.

I looked at my phone. It was 5:25 a.m. Which is too early to be freaked out about someone not showing up, but we usually met at five, and this had never happened before.

I texted him. *Where are you?*

No response. My gut started to feel a little queasy.

Five minutes later, I texted again: . . . ?

Nothing came back. My gut twisted, and I slowly got up and brought Griffin, who was confused about what happened to his walk, inside. I went back to bed. And I stayed there.

My brain spent the day fuming. How can a person be that close to you, say all those nice things, and then just disappear? That was crueler, in fact, than never having been there in the first place. Why did Daxton have to pretend I mattered, just to make it clear a few weeks later that I didn't?

At three p.m. that afternoon, I decided to text him again. I wrote four different versions:

You better be dead. Nothing else is a good enough excuse

I read it and reread it. Many, many times. My finger hovered over the send button. But then I pictured his smiling eyes, and I erased it.

Nice. Standing me up. Lose my number

I erased it.

I don't have friends who treat me this way

I erased it.

I finally settled on one. It was hard, because I wasn't feeling it. But I sent this:

You okay, Daxton?

I saw the dots right away.

Hey! So sorry. Emergency with my dad. He's ok. His blood sugar went through the roof. At hospital. Scary here! Was gonna text but kinda crazy

This feeling flooded through my chest. Like the opposite of the feeling I had when Nimo disappeared on me. Something like grace. Like, maybe the world wasn't so bad, after all. Like maybe Daxton wasn't such a Normal, or I was one, too. Whatever. We were the same, and that was what mattered.

That's ok! Sorry your dad is sick! Miss you!

I miss you too. We should hang out some night

I texted, *!!! Me? Why in the world would you want to*

I erased it.

Yeah ok. When this is all over for sure. For now, socially distant walks. yay

Nah. I mean yeah. But tonight. 10pm? Come outside. Wear a mask. It'll be ok, I promise. Just need to see you

This shiver went through my entire body, and I smiled like I hadn't in a long time.

Ok

———

That night, at ten, I leashed up Griffin. My mom was asleep, passed out after a long, terrible day at Banner Health. I left her a note in case she woke up, but I knew she wouldn't.

The hot night air made the hairs on my arms tingle as I crept out our front door. It wasn't exactly like I was going out to go clubbing, or anything illicit, really. But I felt shaky and undeniably alive anyway, because I knew he'd be there.

And he was.

Sitting on the artificial-grass lawn across the street, just far enough away from the streetlight that he wouldn't catch anyone's attention if they peeked out the window or drove by. But nobody was doing that. Not at ten p.m., not in this neighborhood, and not at this time, when the world was on an extended time-out. Squirrel sat, obedient and perfect, by his side.

I sat down on our concrete driveway, right across from him, my heart surging like a criminal or a thief, and also like someone who was—maybe?—on the way to being in love.

How would I even know?

Griffin perched next to me, not quite as obedient and perfect, but good enough. He leaned into me.

I gave a little wave, and Daxton waved back. I could see his black mask just barely, his face even less. His body was just a hint of a shape, long and thin and lovely.

He very softly, very deliberately put his hand on his knee.

I put my hand on my knee, too.

He reached his hand out toward me, as if we could hold hands, if our arms were both fifty feet long. My whole body shook with joy.

I stuck my hand out too, and I caressed his through the air. And in that way, we held each other.

One Day

by Sajni Patel

Quarantine *sucked*. Especially when we were packed into urban apartments like a package of Oreos, and not even the interesting kind of Oreos, but the strange flavor that no one liked. There was no space, no quiet.

All day, my parents worked in the living room. *All day,* my little sister, Lilly, cohosted her summer school virtual classroom, that little teacher's pet. She learned how to mute everyone in the first session and had gone dictator with power ever since.

"I decide who talks now," she said in this weird, deranged voice, pressing a finger against the keyboard on my old laptop. She took up the entire dining table with her craft supplies. I mean, when had arts become so cutthroat? I could not with her.

Lilly was probably negotiating Clorox wipes and toilet paper on the elementary school black market in exchange for electronics. If she were the mastermind behind an entire underground network, no one would be surprised, and my parents would probably reward her with the rarely seen fresh donut.

I rolled my eyes, grabbed a piece of sourdough (because baking as a family was our thing now), and went to the bedroom I shared with Lilly. It was big enough for two twin beds, two nightstands, one dresser, and two desks. Every surface was covered with snacks. There were various bags of chips and cookie containers on the floor. Half-eaten bags of all four flavors of Teddy Grahams in empty popcorn bowls. Just looking at the soda bottles in the corner made my stomach hurt. Yet I still stuffed my face.

I plopped onto my bed, which I hadn't made in who knows how long, and felt something hard slide beneath my hand as I eased back against the pillows.

"What the . . ." I snatched the controller headset. "So that's where you went. Been looking for you since last week." Now I could finally get back to playing video games with the girls and talk about . . . bread. Marly and Janice were also baking a lot these days. Marly had gotten into sewing super cute handmade masks, and Janice had added TikTok videos to her repertoire, which seemed more productive than whatever I was doing.

I was too bored to play. And I had a terrible stabby headache from all the screen time and noise. I just wanted to nap.

Lilly's voice carried through the hallway as she told someone named Matthew to raise his virtual hand if he wanted to talk or she'd mute him indefinitely. Then there was shuffling feet and movement and a closing door. Ma had walked into her room to her desk, which was directly behind my bed. Her muffled voice permeated the wall and went straight into my throbbing head. And Dad was on a lunch break by the sound of clanking pots and pans.

Ugh. I just wanted peace and quiet, no noise, no screens, no talking. There was always something happening from seven in the morning to ten at night. Meetings, classes, TV, cooking, cleaning, texting, talking, and even religious virtual gatherings.

I was losing. My. Mind. If it were possible to crawl out of my skin and escape into the clouds, I *so* would. Luckily there was a place I could escape to. My one refuge in this miserably confined, loud-as-crap world.

The balcony.

Ma was too worried about bioterrorism (aka some infected a-hole purposely coughing on us) to let us go on walks without her and Dad. But the balcony was safe.

Crawling out the window and onto the balcony, I sat outside on a folding chair four stories up. The balcony was small, partially filled with plants I'd desperately tried to grow.

"Just *live*," I told them. But they didn't seem very interested in cooperating in the muggy, summer heat. Poor roses wilted with sad, decrepit petals, and mint dried up into crispy strings.

I sighed and closed my eyes. The tall buildings kept the sunlight from directly searing my face and cast shade instead.

A light breeze shifted through the air and caressed my skin. Thank goodness for shorts and thin shirts.

Beautiful, blissful quiet.

Brum. Brum. BRRRRRRUM.

What *was* that twangy, guttural pitch? Vibrations of something hit the air and pierced my precious silence. My stabby headache was getting agitated AF.

The sound got louder and louder until I pried open an eye and searched the balconies for the source of this . . . this racket. And then I found him. Across the wide alley, some dude in a gray T-shirt and blue board shorts sat on his balcony the next building over, one floor below, and two balconies over. His head bent low as he played a guitar. A mass of thick black hair that needed a haircut fell over his face.

I gritted my teeth and hoped he would stop soon. But he didn't. I glanced at my window, but there were a hundred more annoying sounds inside.

"Hey!" I shouted, cringing at the loudness. Stabby headache was going to kill me.

He didn't hear. Dude was playing that thing like nothing else, like no one else was around. When in reality, several hundred people lived in these two buildings and I couldn't possibly be the only one wanting quiet time.

Jumping to my feet, I shouted again, my voice scratching my throat. He paused and scanned the building until he found me glaring at him, my hands on my hips, and standing against the railing.

He waved.

I didn't wave back. "Can you stop? I'm trying to get some quiet," I yelled down to him, cringing from the pain in my head.

He shrugged and mouthed, *Sorry*. Then he went back to playing his guitar. It sounded even louder. The audacity! Did he think he just owned the air?

I needed something. I turned one way and then the other, looking for something to throw. I was heated. My skin prickled and a fire whooshed down the back of my neck. I couldn't throw one of my sickly plants. My mom had bought those pots, and they might shatter onto someone below. In a moment of temperamental spontaneity, I tugged off my sneaker and chucked it at him with the aim and force of a seasoned softball pitcher.

As soon as the shoe left my fingers, I yelped. Gah! Oh, no! Why did I do that! Was this assault? Did I hurt him? Had I lost my favorite shoe?

I ducked just as my sneaker hit the brick side of his building. He carefully stood to find me with my hands on my face and my fingers slightly opening to peer through.

He pressed his lips together and frowned. He shook his head like he was about to call my mom and tell her what I'd done. My mom would ground me, for sure. Well, like ground me after quarantine was lifted because right now it didn't matter. My entire life was one long, weird grounding session.

He bent down, swept up the shoe, and tossed it in the air a few times as if he were debating throwing it back at me.

Ew. He picked up my sneaker without sanitizing it?

In the end, he saluted me with my own shoe and mouthed, *Thanks.*

Um. I kinda needed my shoe back, though. I wriggled one socked foot in horror. That wasn't just any sneaker. It was one half to a glorious pair of white Converse made special by my friends. Ya know, the ones whom I may never ever see again in an actual school.

He returned to playing that hollow sound, to *irritating* me. I waved my arms wildly in the air to get his attention, but he just smirked and bobbed his head and got really into his music. I yelled at him again but ended up straining my voice and coughing.

"Beta?" Dad opened my bedroom door and walked to the window. "What are you doing? Who are you yelling at?"

"Some person who's making too much noise," I said weakly, my throat hurting from all the yelling.

He tilted his head, listened, and smiled. "Nice music. Sort of relaxing, no? Come inside and eat lunch. We have sourdough sandwiches."

I groaned. If I ate one more slice of bread, I was going to turn into a loaf. I grunted at Guitar Boy and crawled inside.

Lunch was as peaceful as things could get these days, mainly because our mouths were busy chewing. During meals, we always kept the TV off and electronics were left on charging stations. Before quarantine, we talked about our feelings and our day while we ate, but we were so up in each other's business now that there was no need to. *Privacy? What's that?*

"Zoom meetings leave a buzz in my head," Ma told Dad.

"It's the earbuds," he said. "Necessary and inevitable."

She had a glazed look and mumbled, "I might need a drink tonight."

"Can I sleep in the living room again?" Lilly asked as she munched on carrots.

"Sure, beta," Ma said.

What a relief. Lilly sleeping in the living room beneath a makeshift tent with her stuffed animals and her friends on FaceTime gave me a room to myself. It was the *best*.

When we finished lunch, I cleaned the kitchen. Then I showered. All the while, plotting ways to get my shoe back. When I emerged from the bathroom, I spotted the dry-erase board against the wall. Hmmm. What if . . .

"Are you using the dry-erase board?" I asked Lilly.

"You may use," she said.

"Thanks." I grabbed the board, an eraser, and a black dry-erase marker and went onto the balcony.

Guitar Boy had left. I spotted my sneaker behind his chair. For now, I enjoyed the solace.

—

With my head finally void of buzz, thoughts, worries, and anxieties, the headache eased away. An hour of quiet had been magnificent. Until Guitar Boy came back out.

I glared at him, silently daring him to play with what I'd hoped were squinted eyes of doom. He waved, sat down, faced me, and strummed.

First thing first. I held up my sign.

I NEED MY SHOE BACK

He kept playing but squinted to read. Then shrugged.

LIKE NOW

He held a hand up to his ear in the shape of a phone.

I JUST WANT MY SHOE!!!

He pulled out his phone with a grin. A very cute, albeit impish, one. Then he held it up to me and waited.

Gah!

NOT GIVING YOU MY #!!

He shrugged like no biggie, placed the shoe in front of him, and . . . serenaded it. His music was moving, little rain-drops on my soul, his fingers adept and so different from the noise he had bombarded me with earlier. I was at a loss for dry-erase words. And apparently, I was not alone.

Several people came out onto their balconies and listened, applauding when he stopped. I found myself leaning on my elbows against the railing, unwillingly mesmerized by the resonating, majestic notes from songs I didn't recognize.

Guitar Boy played for a while longer, then sat around with my shoe, all the while ignoring my many adamant signs.

This went on for the rest of the evening with intervals for bathroom and dinner breaks as he toyed with my sneaker. After every song, he held his hand to his ear in the shape of a phone. Every time, I shook my head with as much annoyance as I could show.

At first, everyone else minded their own business. But his music, or our quarrel, or whatever led to a gradually increasing balcony audience. People got nosy, wanting to know what our tiff was about and why I didn't want to talk to him when he was essentially serenading me. One person, then another, then a few more, cried out, "Oh, come on!" "Give the poor boy a break!" "Give him your number!" "How romantic!" "What music!"

Romantic? No. Opportunistic? Yes.

He played into the night. Maybe I could bide time. How long would he last? How long before his back hurt and his fingers bled?

"That's lovely music. Who's playing?" Ma asked as she walked through my room.

I went inside. "Some guy who won't let me have quiet," I grumbled.

"Ah, beta. Come watch a movie with us," she said instead and went into the living room with Lilly's pillows and blanket.

"Maybe." But all I really wanted to do was figure out how to get my shoe back.

—

Strange that the first thing to pop into my head as soon as I woke up the next morning was not having to pee or what to eat for breakfast, or even the realization of blissful morning peace, but Guitar Boy. After going through my morning routine and doing some reading, I went outside.

There he was. Sitting on his chair, facing me. He waved.

Without breaking eye contact, I held up my sign.

SHOE!

He held up my sneaker in one hand and his phone in the other. A dozen scenarios gushed through my brain. Could I throw a pot at him? Could I climb up to his balcony and take my shoe while he was gone? Could I figure out which apartment was his and knock on the door and tell his mom what he'd been doing?

Guitar Boy played smooth, soft notes for almost an hour, a new song each time.

We took breaks and came back out to continue our standoff.

In the evening when more people got home, as well as other kids, they'd come out to listen and take sides and add irritating commotion. Except those who took my side, of course. They got imaginary brownies for being on side *ME*.

This went on for another day. The division of sides quickly shifted. More people turned into Team Guitar Boy. I was losing the battle.

—

While Marly posted IG stories of her cats dressed in tutus and hand-knit caps, and Janice group-texted us her new monthly workout challenge for that better booty, I complained about Guitar Boy. Today's standoff included snacks on the balcony, shades for high noon, a fan, a pillow for my back, an icy fruit drink, and my trusty sign that Lilly would need back any minute now for a summer school presentation (!!). Guitar Boy was equipped with a bottle of water and his own snacks. We pretty much lived out here now.

He played. Always slow and melodious, sucking me into a trance with songs I'd never heard. His music lured me into a daze, one that I had fought against all this time and wanted to be upset over. But over the course of these past days, it had created something sorta bizarre. I hadn't noticed it until now, until I fully gave in. Because one: being annoyed added to my headache. Two: his music was kind of soothing. Three: this was a free show, to be honest.

I'd lost track of time as everything around me melted and blurred. It didn't matter how hot it was, or if my butt hurt from sitting in this folding chair. Musical notes fell around this backstreet width of space between us. Notes that ballooned into plump, swaying raindrops and dancing fairies of round, thrumming beats.

For once, noise didn't give me a stabby headache, or induce anxiety, or make me want to throw something.

Was this what music did for him? All cathartic and stuff?

This time when he stopped, there was a void. Silence was too . . . quiet. I actually missed his music. Badly. Like absolute hollowness. In a world full of colors and chaos, there was now a splattered goop of a black abyss with a sign that read *You Are Here.*

I went inside and cooked dinner for my family, giving Lilly the task of measuring ingredients. My parents had taken a nap earlier and now were folding laundry.

"You two need to make your beds and clean your room," Ma scolded.

"Okay," we told her.

"Honestly. We need routine and cleanliness. We don't want ants, do we?"

Dinner came and went. Then Lilly and I cleaned our room. Well, I did most of it. She put away her things but I made the beds and cleaned up all the snacks. She immediately went to the living room for movie night, which was every night.

I went onto the balcony, ready for the standoff during the seven p.m. serenade, but surprisingly found several people on their balconies around us, all quiet, like they were waiting for something. Guitar Boy didn't have his guitar out. He waved.

One by one, people across the balconies held up signs—on

paper shopping bags, on dry-erase boards, on Amazon cardboard boxes—imploring me to give the guy a chance. And with those signs came hoots and hollers cheering me on.

Guitar Boy just stood there, his hands shoved into his jeans pockets, a smirk on his face, and a shrug as if he hadn't orchestrated this entire stunt.

Heat rushed to my cheeks. I groaned and yelled, "Fine!" But in reality, giddiness squirmed through me. Never had a boy tried so long and this hard to get my number. Never had one put together a phone number proposal like this or had an entire crowd backing him up. Had a boy ever even asked for my number?

The scattered crowd applauded and whistled. Thank goodness my family was in the living room watching a movie turned on so loud that they hadn't heard this commotion.

I didn't have the dry-erase board, so I held up my fingers to hand over my cellphone number one number at a time. Guitar Boy immediately added it to his phone as my face warmed from all the approving attention.

I expected my phone to buzz with a text. But nah. It rang. He actually called me! Right here and now in front of everyone!

My hands shook as I answered.

"Hi," he said in a level, deep voice as he stuffed one hand back into his pocket.

I tried not to smile, but dang it! I was grinning so hard that I almost spun around so he wouldn't see.

"Hey," I said as casually as possible, but my voice might've been trembling.

"So this is what you sound like. When you're not yelling."

"Yep."

"Thanks for giving me your number."

My gaze fluttered to the alley below, away from his intense look, away from the nosy audience. "You forced me to. Did you tell all these people to do this?"

"What? That? Had nothing to do with it."

I glanced at him and could see he was grinning now. "Right. This just evolved on its own?"

He laughed. Wow. He sounded so nice. My skin tingled.

"Can I have my shoe back?" I asked.

"I dunno . . ."

"Wasn't that the entire point of getting my number?"

"No. The point was to finally talk to you. If I give you your shoe back, you might not talk to me again."

"So, extortion, is it?"

"Collateral."

"Wow. Okay. Can I ever expect to get my shoe back?"

"Of course." He looked behind him. "I have to go. Can I text you later?"

"Do I have a choice if you're holding my shoe hostage?"

He held up the sneaker for me to see. "It's in good hands. Promise."

I clamped down on a smile as he went inside. And with his departure, I went inside, too. I joined my family for movie night, if nothing else to get my mind off Guitar Boy, but found myself constantly checking my phone.

Which didn't go unnoticed by Ma. "Waiting for something important?"

"Someone is supposed to text me."

"Someone? Not a specific name? Are you talking to boys?" Ma asked.

"Whaaaaat?" I said without much conviction.

"Nice thing about quarantine is that I don't have to worry about boys getting too close to you. The virus took care of that! Six feet apart at all times! Hard to kiss or do things you shouldn't be doing when you have to maintain social distancing."

"Ugh. Can we not talk about that? No one is trying to get close to me."

The movie ended and still no text.

Lilly was already asleep in bed. I crawled underneath my covers, facing the wall with my back to my little sister. The window was in my view and the phone beside my face so that I could see it light up.

This was totally uncool to wait for some boy. I was not here for this. I was going to sleep and respond when I responded.

Just as my eyelids fluttered closed, the screen lit up.

Guitar Boy: Hey. Are you still awake?

I tapped the phone, deliberating on replying.

Me: Yeah

Guitar Boy: My name's Neal. What's your name?

Me: Bobby

Guitar Boy: Bobby? Isn't that a boy's name?

Me: Not in my culture. Don't throw your social constructs at me

Guitar Boy: LOL. Fair

Me: I need my shoe back

Guitar Boy: Do you though?

Me: Yes!

Guitar Boy: When you threw it at me, thought it was a gift

Me: At least I didn't hit you

Guitar Boy: That would've hurt. You threw it kinda hard. Nice aim, BTW

Me: I'm a softball pitcher. I could've thrown it way harder

Guitar Boy: Nice! I mean the pitcher part. Glad you didn't throw harder

Me: You could be a gentleman and throw my shoe back

Guitar Boy: I don't have your aim. It might end up on someone else's balcony

Me: Meet me outside, then

Guitar Boy: Sounds like an invitation to a fight

Me: Listen. I also have a softball bat and I'm not afraid to throw it

Guitar Boy: I'm going to hold on to your shoe for a little longer

Me: :/

Guitar Boy: Collateral. Hey, can we video chat?

Me: Why?

Guitar Boy: So I can see your face

Me: You saw me outside

Guitar Boy: Kinda far, though

Me: I'm in bed and it's dark. You're not going to see much

Guitar Boy: I'll take what I can get

I bit my lip and thought about the request for a moment before obliging. But mainly because I wanted to see him closer up, too. I popped in my earbuds and checked how I looked on camera first. Eh. It wasn't the best, but it was dark and he wouldn't be able to see much of me. I took in a deep, nervous breath and video called him.

Within seconds, Neal manifested on my screen. He sat in

bed in a well-lit room, his cheeks a little flushed as if maybe he was nervous, too. He had a lot of quarantine hair, wavy and wild, that curled at the ends. It brushed his ears and forehead. His smile squished up his intense, brown eyes, and deep dimples formed. But his smile! He had this big, bright, dazzling smile behind full lips.

He was *super* cute! I mean . . . Mena Massoud, was that you??

Neal grinned. "You gonna stare any harder? You might hit your face on the screen."

I swallowed. "Whatever. Anyone tell you that you look like Mena Massoud?"

He raised an eyebrow. "Who?"

"The guy who played Aladdin?"

He shook his head and pressed his lips together. Those dimples! "Um. No."

"Oh. Well, you do. Anyway."

He furrowed his brows and brought his phone closer to his face. "Who is that behind you?"

I jumped and rolled over, almost screaming with fright. "Lilly!" I quietly yelled, trying to get my heart to calm down.

She, like a little creeper, was standing over me and just all in my business. "Are you talking to a *boy*?"

"Shhh! What are you doing? You scared me to death."

"You're not supposed to be talking to boys. Who is that?" She leaned down to look at my screen and excitedly asked, "Is that Aladdin?"

Neal laughed and waved.

"Oh my god," I muttered, and ushered her away. "Go back to bed."

Then I said to Neal, "I gotta go."

—

I'd showered, washed my hair, and shaved, just in case . . . ya know, Neal wanted to video call. What if I accidentally dropped my phone and he got a look at hairy legs? I checked out my reflection. Ew. This growth on unkempt brows. I deftly plucked my eyebrows and made sure my clothes were fresh and clean.

"Since when have you begun drinking coffee?" Ma asked as I poured a mug for myself in the kitchen and grabbed a waffle hot out of the toaster. I smothered it with butter, no syrup.

"Just want something not sweet. My gums are starting to hurt."

She frowned. "Yes. We need to limit sugar. Quarantine is not an excuse to go sugar wild."

"Where are you off to in a hurry?" Dad asked as he helped Lilly with something on the laptop.

"Going to eat breakfast on the balcony."

"Good to get some fresh air. Make sure to water those poor plants while you're out there."

"Okay." I closed the bedroom door and hurried to the balcony, throwing a pillow and my sweatshirt out to make myself as comfy as possible.

Everything was set up, my shades on, relaxed and leaned back on my pillow-cushioned folding chair with coffee in hand and half-eaten waffle on a paper towel on my lap.

In about four minutes, Neal texted.

Guitar Boy: Hi! I'm going to be out on the balcony in a bit if you want to come out. Some real-time face time? Maybe?

Me: Sure

When he emerged, he beamed and waved. Then he leaned his forearms against the railing and we just watched each other. There was something very rewarding about being able to check out a boy from afar. And the shades hid my gawking now that I knew what he looked like close up. There was an entire conversation between us without uttering a single word.

He eventually sat down and pulled a book from the windowsill before asking for a video call.

Sure. Why not?

My stomach tied into little knots in anticipation as his image appeared on my phone. The shades stayed on, though.

"Hi," he said, simple but so thrilling. He was even cuter in the daylight, his skin glowing.

"Hey," I replied, trying to sound as chill as possible.

"Whatcha up to today?"

"Oh, you know? The usual. Eating, drinking, watching my friends' TikToks. I might play a game with my fam later. Waiting for a certain boy to hand over my shoe."

He chuckled, sending a pleasant flutter through my belly. Wow. *Calm down, woman.*

"Why'd you throw it at me in the first place?" he asked.

"I needed quiet and the balcony is the only place I can find it. I asked you to stop. You ignored me."

"Ah. But throwing something at me was kinda extreme."

"With everything going on in quarantine, all the noise, being stuck inside, glued to screens, I was getting bad headaches and just needed quiet. I shouldn't have thrown anything at you."

He knitted his brows. "I'm sorry. I probably added to that stress."

"At first, definitely."

"Not anymore?"

"I think the music you play actually helps."

He nodded. "It helps me."

"You're stressed, too?"

"Who isn't? Worried. Bored. Irritated. Playing the guitar helps."

"Where did you learn how to play?"

"YouTube. Gotten much better since quarantine, though. It's harder to play songs already out there, so I just make up my own stuff, sometimes."

I chewed the inside of my cheek. "It's really nice. Thanks for sharing your music with me."

"Anytime. I can be quiet, too, though, if you need."

"Thanks. So. What are you up to?"

He held up the book. "Summer reading. Dinner with my

mom later. Maybe indoor workout. Play some music. Consider returning a certain shoe later."

He reached over to grab my sneaker. "What's up with the scribbles, though?"

"Those are not scribbles."

He made a face. "Are we talking about the same shoe?"

I sighed, longing for the other half of my white sneakers with colorfully inked words and drawings. "When the pandemic hit up north, we had a feeling that it wasn't going to just end and life be normal after spring break. We knew it would hit us, too. Kinda saw it coming when school sent us home early for spring break and told us not to come back until further notice, especially when other states were going into quarantine. Anyway, my friends and I bought shoes before we got quarantined, and we signed them and wrote little doodles and pictures and . . . um . . . yeah, fine scribbles."

I'd expected him to laugh or mock me for such a child-ish, girl thing to do. Instead he half smiled, the right corner of his lips arching upward in a perpetually adorable, dimple-inducing look. "That's pretty awesome. Wish we'd thought of that. Was it your idea?"

"Yeah. Definitely got into trouble with my parents for *ruining* brand-new shoes," I said. "So . . . what are you doing all summer, besides holding shoes hostage?"

"TikTok videos."

"Of what? Playing the guitar?"

He seemed a little embarrassed. "Dancing."

I gasped. "To what? I want to see."

"Nope."

"Um, yes. You can't keep my shoe and not give anything in return."

He tried to change the subject to summer quarantine hobbies, but I kept reeling the conversation back. He relented. And I spent the rest of the day watching, rewatching, and triple-watching some hilarious, amazing, and swoon-worthy videos.

I, of course, shared with Marly and Janice, who conceded with all the heart-eyed emojis that Guitar Boy was the absolute cutest boy ever. Oh, and also a good dancer.

After dinner, I'd stayed up late on the balcony while Neal played, this time airy and uplifting.

This is for you, he'd texted.

Was a boy seriously playing music just for me? Well, nosy neighbors thought so, but they also benefited because they sure did stay out and enjoyed with me. Applause ensued after every song. Neal even took a bow. He'd earned it, and I absolutely saw how music had become his outlet.

That night, I video chatted with Neal for another hour. In the dark. Completely alone. But for the first time in a long time, not really alone at all.

—

The next morning, my parents left early for the weekly grocery run. It was a whole event now. The carefully calculated and long list that had accumulated over the past seven days, the drive, the masks and hand sanitizer and wipes, the waiting in line outside the store, the social distancing protocol within the store, and of course the long checkout process, all the while praying they could find everything in one place. Not to mention having to wipe everything down once we unloaded groceries inside.

"Can you come outside?" Neal asked over the phone.

"For my shoe?"

"Yes."

I frowned. "Does that mean you're willing to give up the one thing that ensures we keep talking?"

"I hope we keep talking afterward, with or without a hostage. Meet you in front of the buildings in ten minutes? I just have to finish this sauce."

"You cook?"

"Yep. I don't have much else to do. Been watching YouTube cooking videos. But now my mom complains that *she* doesn't have anything to do," he said.

"What are you making?"

"Fettucine alfredo with veggies. Just missing bread, though. Store has been out. Thought of trying to make my own bread, but it looks hard. Plus the store is always out of flour, anyway. Guess everyone is baking," he muttered in this sad, disappointed voice.

"We hoarded that stuff early, before quarantine was official."

"Smart."

I chewed on my lower lip and finally said, "See you in ten."

"Awesome."

I hurried to change into something cute and decided on a red tank top and navy blue shorts. I checked my reflection in the dresser mirror. Ew. Was that a pimple on my jaw and what was going on with this frizzy hair?

Agh! I couldn't meet a boy for the first time looking like this! I whipped my hair into a top bun.

In the kitchen, I grabbed a Ziploc bag prepacked with Clorox wipes and stuffed it into my back pocket. In the corner of my eye, I noticed the loaf of bread that we'd made the other day. We hadn't even cut into it, and it was the prettiest one by far. The X cut on top was pure pro-level, the crust crispy and golden brown, and the inside sure to be as chewy as its misshapen counterparts.

I carefully wrapped it in foil and then placed it in a bag when Lilly came out of the bathroom.

"Are you going outside?" she asked, her brown eyes wide and accusatory.

"Don't tell." I held a finger to my lips.

But Lilly wasn't having it. She was one of those little formidable girls who was going to grow into a formidable woman. She didn't have to say anything, just gave me a look that said, *You're not going without me or I'm telling.*

I sighed and dropped my head back. "Fine. Be quick."

She ran to our room and then skipped back to the foyer with a face mask on and a loaded water gun in hand. We slipped into flip-flops as I adjusted my own face mask. We headed out, through the long hallway and down the stairs.

The sun hit my legs as soon as we reached the sidewalk.

With no one around, I heaved out a breath, closed my eyes, and just enjoyed the sun, the space, the outdoors.

A few moments later, Neal walked out of his apartment building and headed toward us, stopping several feet in front of me. He wore the heck out of knee-length cargo shorts and black T-shirt with a matching mask. Ugh! Boys following quarantine precautions and wearing face masks were so snackable.

His hair looked absolutely touchable in person. Too bad the mask hid his dimples. But he smiled, because his eyes crinkled, and OMG, who on this planet looked so adorable in a quarantine mask?

"You got my shoe?" I asked.

He tossed my sneaker a few times into the air before gingerly tossing it to me. I stepped aside and let it hit the ground.

"You missed," he said.

"Um, no." With the bag looped around my wrist, I whipped out a Clorox wipe and sanitized the shoe. Then left it on the sidewalk to air-dry for the recommended four minutes. Then cleaned my hands with sanitizer.

Neal rolled his eyes. But then he pulled out a small bottle of hand sanitizer and cleaned his hands, too. How was that not like the sexiest thing right now? A guy who took this whole thing as seriously as we did?

He took a few steps and Lilly immediately jumped beside me and aimed her water gun at Neal, pumping it a few times.

"Six feet apart!" she demanded.

He stopped, holding his hands up. "Yes, ma'am."

"My little sister, Lilly," I said off his look.

"She's cute."

Lilly frowned. "There's nothing cute about social distancing."

Neal's shoulders shook, as if he were trying not to laugh. "You're right," he said. "This is very serious. Awesome job keeping the family safe."

"You're taller than I thought," I said.

"You're exactly what I thought," he replied.

"Thanks for returning my shoe. I mean, for doing the right thing, which you could've done days ago."

He shook his head. "But then you would've never given me your number."

"Extortion." I glanced at my sneaker and noticed a new scribble.

Neal had doodled a guitar with notes beside it in blue Sharpie and had signed his name at the bottom. Beneath the *E* and *A* of his name, he added an upward curve so that the letters looked like eyes with a smile beneath and yes, even dimples to make sure I didn't forget who Neal was. I found myself grinning hard.

"You signed it?"

"Hope you don't mind," he said, his brows furrowed, maybe worried.

"It's . . ." Amazing. Charming. Sweet. "Nice."

"Let's go play!" Lilly said in a high-pitched whine cutting through our moment. She hadn't been allowed outside without the parents in a while, and she was probably frothing at the mouth to run wild.

I groaned. "We have to get back inside before our parents get home from grocery shopping. Have to help wipe everything down."

Neal nodded. "Yeah. I better get home, too. Have to finish cooking."

"Here. This is for you." I dangled the bag in front of him so he could grab it from the bottom.

He took it cautiously. "What's this?"

"Bread."

He regarded me for a few seconds.

"We make a lot of bread," I explained. "It's our family time thing. It's sourdough. Took lots of tries to get it right, but my dad mastered sourdough starter."

He looked at the bag in the most unexpected, perplexed, but appreciative way. "Are your parents going to be mad that you gave away food?"

"No. We still have bread left. Besides. You don't have flour to make your own bread because people like us hoarded it. Now you can have bread with your pasta."

He smiled big by the way his eyes squished up above his mask. I'd do anything to see those dimples. "I'd hug you if I could."

My belly did flips until Lilly reminded us, "Six feet apart!"

"Right. Which is why I won't. But maybe one day," he said, hopeful.

I bit my lip. "Yeah. One day."

One day, quarantine would be lifted.

One day, we'd be able to get within six feet and not need face masks and I'd be able to see his dimples in person.

One day, we'd stand right beside each other, his skin brushing mine, sparks coming to life, our fingers twitching as we slowly touched pinkies.

One day, we'd hold hands and not worry about sending anyone to the hospital.

One day, we'd hug and I would feel his heartbeat with my cheek against his chest.

One day, his arms would wrap around me and I'd smell him and feel safe.

One day, we would get to hang out, go to the movies, meet friends.

One day, he'd invite me over and play the guitar.

One day, I'd tell him that his music had soothed my anxiety and our balcony romance made me feel normal, special, *human* again.

One day, we might even kiss and it would be beyond amazing.

"One day" couldn't come soon enough, but it would come. I couldn't *wait* for our "one day."

The Rules of Comedy

by Auriane Desombre

The millennials have taken over TikTok.

I don't know who invited them, or why they came, or why they think making jokes about the phrase *per my last email* is so damn funny, but here they are, all over my main feed, ruining my favorite app. Can't they all go back to Instagram or wherever else they came from?

I drop my phone onto the couch and meander to the kitchen, where I pour myself a bowl of Cinnamon Toast Crunch for my third lunch. Eve reaches across the kitchen island to snatch some out of my bowl before I pour in the milk, and I toss her the (now mostly empty) box.

"Hands off my snacks, please."

She grins at me, swallowing. "Respect the older sister privileges, Harper, please."

I snatch my bowl off the counter before she can reach for it again. Since she came home from NYU when they closed because of the pandemic, we've been running seriously low on all the good snacks. I grab a bag of pretzels out of the pantry on my way back to the living room to squirrel it away for later.

Eve follows me, the box of cereal propped up in her arms like a newborn baby. Smush, our family's squashy pug, tips his head up when he hears the bag crinkle. I toss him a cereal from my bowl, and he almost catches it. It lands on the floor instead, and he does an accidental backflip as he tumbles off the couch in his eagerness to go after it.

Eve runs to fix his inside-out ear. I watch her go, biting back a laugh at Smush's confused expression.

This is exactly the kind of thing I'd use to start a conversation with Alyssa Sanderson during group work in bio. We're the only ninth-graders in the class, so Mr. Ray always lets us be in the same lab group. I used the time wisely. I'd tell her about the way Smush flopped onto the floor, tipping myself sideways in my desk chair to try and make her laugh, to let her nose to wrinkle up as her eyes brighten.

Her laugh is really cute. Plus, she's the second-funniest person I know, after Eve, and every time I can get her to laugh feels like a win.

But we never really got from in-the-same-class friends to texting-after-school friends, so I haven't talked to her since school closed.

Eve looks down at me, Smush flopped in her arms, his

tongue lolling upside-down at me. I boop him on the nose, and he nips at my thumb.

"You okay?" Eve asks.

I tilt my head back, groaning. "No."

She shifts Smush's weight against her hip so she can free one hand to tug the end of my braid. "What's wrong?"

I shrug. "I miss my friends."

Especially my not-quite-close-enough-to-text-just-'cause friend. My overanalyze-her-wardrobe-in-a-desperate-attempt-to-see-if-she's-gay friend.

My wish-we-weren't-"friends" friend.

Eve narrows her eyes at me. "You FaceTimed Anna for three hours this morning."

"Are you suggesting I only have one friend?" I cross my arms over my chest.

She raises an eyebrow at me.

"Okay, fine, I only have one friend—starting a new high school with social anxiety is hard, okay?"

But what Eve didn't realize is I did have a few friends who were just not in the close-enough-to-FaceTime variety. Anna and I have been best friends since elementary school. We're so comfortable with each other that we can spend hours hanging out on video calls, even if we run out of things to say. Yesterday, I watched her make banana bread while I tried unsuccessfully to curl my hair for the first time, all in companionable silence.

A teasing smile flashes across Eve's face. "So who are you really missing?"

Heat creeps across my cheeks, and I get up to wash my bowl—and hide the fact that my face is turning red to match. Eve follows me, doing a little dance with Smush.

"No one."

Eve gives a disbelieving laugh.

"Harper's in love, Harper's in looove," she sings as she swings Smush around in a waltz.

I drop my bowl into the drying rack on the counter. "Don't you have homework to do?"

"I'm procrastinating."

"They don't work you hard enough in comedy school."

She purses her lips at me. "Now you sound like Mom. I do not go to *comedy school*, I'm majoring in film so I can *write* comedy for—"

She puts Smush down so she can talk with her hands, launching into her favorite rant. It's an all-too-familiar one since she declared a major in film and TV, especially now that she's about to finish her junior year and Mom has spent the entire month since NYU sent students home hounding her about career prospects. Once she's in full rant mode, she'll tire herself out before she can remember to pester me about my crush.

—

I'm supposed to be doing math homework, but my textbook lies facedown on the fluffy white carpet next to me. I'm instead sprawled out on the floor, staring at Alyssa's latest Snapchat story, my head propped up on the couch leg. I have no idea how to do the work, nor do I have any desire to figure it out. Especially because Alyssa just posted a snap story makeup tutorial that's both hilarious and cute, which is extremely unfair. How am I supposed to focus on anything else?

But then I hear my mom's footsteps coming down the hall. I snatch open my bio textbook at random and flip it onto my stomach just as she emerges into the living room.

"Studying?" she asks.

My eyes sweep over my homework. I truly have no idea how any of this works, but I nod anyway, and she gives me an approving smile.

Breathing out a sigh of relief, I wait until she's disappeared into the kitchen before I pick up my phone again. I tap right to Alyssa's name in my contacts. I have her number from when we had to work on a lab together outside of class, and our chat history is depressingly limited to schoolwork.

Hey! Do you get any of this bio hw?

I hit send before I can think about it, but that doesn't stop my brain from thinking anyway when the *delivered* notification pops up under my blue bubble of text. *Oh god oh god oh god why?* Did I seriously just ask her about *homework*? I cringe. So transparent, yet so not flirty.

Still, I spend more time over the next hour checking my phone instead of doing the math homework, until she finally responds with a picture of her notes from class. I knew my text was cringey, but I still shrivel up inside when she doesn't say anything more. I shoot back a quick *thanks!!* (two *exclamation points, Harp? Seriously?*) and settle back down to finish my homework.

Half an hour later, after I've tried feeding bits of my textbook to an uninterested Smush, I'm back on TikTok. The app has a way of swallowing time whole. My muscles are starting to atrophy when I scroll to the next video in my bottomless feed, and freeze.

The video's already looped back to the beginning before I have a chance to process what I'm seeing. Because it's Alyssa. On my FYP.

Coming out.

To an audience of over a hundred thousand likes, and piles of comments.

The video loops around for a third time, and I recover from my shock enough to feel a smile tugging at the corners of my lips. She announces that she's gay via a snappy choreographed dance that illuminates text in each corner of her video frame as she moves. Her parents are in the background, and while they're confused and trying to follow the steps at first, they all end up tripping and laughing over each other.

The song she's dancing to is going to be stuck in my head for the rest of the day, I think as I let the video loop for a fourth time. I can't help grinning like a total idiot at it, though.

And, if I'm honest, there's a part of me—a small, teeny tiny, very loud part of me—that's singing. *Alyssa is gay.*

Does this mean I have a chance with her? She's known I'm gay ever since I came out last year, after all.

Not if all we text about is homework, I tell myself, shoulders shrinking. I swallow past the anxious bubble that immediately hardens in my throat as I open our text chain. I just texted her about homework. Will this make me look desperate?

I take a deep breath, and type out a message anyway.

Omg you're tiktok famous!! Congrats on coming out

Her response comes almost immediately.

Thanks!! It was so fun lol. Went really well!

It makes my heartbeat thunder so hard I feel it reverberate in my fingertips.

I'm so glad! Here for you if you need anything

Thanks, Harp!

Of course!

I stare at the screen, willing my fingers to keep typing, to say something—*anything*—that would keep the conversation going, but I draw a blank. Before I can think of anything, she gives my text a heart reaction, and just like that, the conversation is dead.

I drop my phone back onto the floor and sit up straighter. I can't text her about homework again. I've already initiated two conversations with her today.

I switch back to TikTok, trying to get my mind off Alyssa and her vibrant laugh when I remember how many likes she got. How funny her video is, how effortlessly she brings smiles to other people's faces. Even strangers scrolling past her video have laughed, liked, commented on how much her humor got to them. How am I supposed to get her attention now?

I stare at my phone for ages, my chin resting in my palm. I'm desperately reaching for an idea. I try staring off into space, pacing in tight circles around my math textbook, even scrolling through TikTok for inspiration. Instead, I spend hours thinking *Why didn't I think of that?* every time a video makes me laugh.

Eventually, I make a video about my math homework murdering me. My gut sinks as I watch it loop after I post it to my account. It doesn't even make *me* laugh.

I check my phone under the table throughout dinner. For the most part, I get away with it, because Mom is busy grilling Eve about her schoolwork.

"Are you looking for internships?" she asks.

I could've sworn they talked about internships last night. Judging from the pinched look on Eve's face, they've been over this several times already. I check my TikTok again while Eve reminds Mom that they've talked about this before.

"I'm just worried, honey," Mom goes on as she scoops some mashed potatoes onto her plate and passes the bowl to me. "It's not too late to look at more practical options. Comedy isn't, well, serious."

I take a mechanical bite of potato as Eve revs up on her in-defense-of-comedy rant again, barely listening. I can see her trying to catch my eye as she starts talking about her writing, but I'm too busy refreshing my TikTok profile to meet her gaze.

Dinner ends, and my video still has absolutely no likes.

By the time I wake up the next morning, I've accrued an astounding three likes. No comments at all, which makes them feel like pity likes at that. Precious few views. There's no way Alyssa will ever see this. I don't even want her to. Even without comparing it to her coming-out video, it's a huge failure.

I run my hands through my hair, tangled after a night of restlessness. All I want is for Alyssa to see that I can be as funny as she is, that I can be worthy of her.

Trouble is, I'm not.

But someone else in this house is.

—

"So you *do* have a crush," Eve says with a smirk.

Smush saves me from responding by dashing to the windows lining the wall in the living room. His paws skitter against the floor, but I can barely hear even that over the deafening roar of his bark. A squirrel has just dashed through the yard, and we'll all be hearing about it for the next half hour.

"Quiet, Smush," I shout. It's hopeless, he hasn't internalized that command yet, but it saves me from looking at Eve's teasing grin.

It does nothing to protect me from her teasing jab in my side. I slap her fingers away.

"It is not a *crush*, it is soul-crushing, heartbreaking, earth-shattering unrequited *love*, thank you very much," I say, thinking of the way she could make the whole class light up with one of her jokes.

"Why do you need me?" Eve asks. "Aren't you supposed to be yourself?"

I bite my lip. That's the traditional advice, but when humor is social currency, and I'm simply not that funny, what am I supposed to do?

"I just need help making some TikTok videos," I say. "I don't have any good ideas, and I need to go viral so I can end up on her page."

"Can't you just text her and ask her if she wants to Face-Time or something?" Eve asks, raising her voice above Smush's fresh round of screaming, this time at a little bird that has apparently posed a life-or-death threat to the perimeter of the house.

I groan. "She's one of the funniest people I know—"

"Ouch."

"I said *one of*." I give Eve my sternest look. "She's too good for me."

Eve reaches over to ruffle my hair, mouth open with what is sure to be a patronizing speech about how untrue that is, so I duck away from her hand.

"Please," I say. "Put that comedy degree to use."

Eve glances over at Smush, who's now clawing at the window in a desperate attempt to hunt down the chipmunk that lives under the stone wall that lines our yard, his one true nemesis.

"You said she likes animals?" she asks.

One TikTok tutorial later, Eve has Smush framed in her phone lens as he runs from one end of the window to the other, tiny tail wagging with urgency as his bark peaks into a high-pitched whine. When she's done narrating his thoughts—Smush apparently knows a lot of swear words—we go outside to track down the chipmunk and get some shots of him poking his head out from between the rocks. Eve isn't satisfied until she films a squirrel scuttle from tree to tree, almost taunting Smush as he weaves in and out of sight.

The end result is hilarious. Eve narrates Smush's thoughts as he tracks down the squirrel, his nemesis for constantly attempting to invade the yard with his army of small birds. I can't help laughing as I watch the video, even though it also makes heat flush into my cheeks. Why couldn't I put together something like this?

I post "this chipmunk is my nemesis" to my account. When I check it again, five minutes later, I almost drop my phone.

It's already hit thousands of likes. More pour in every time I refresh the page.

"Eve," I scream, even though she's only a few feet away from me, her legs propped up on the end of the couch. "Eve, you did it."

I toss her my phone, and she smiles so wide, I'm worried her lips will crack. "Wow, this is actually doing well."

She reaches over to give me a high five, and I slap her hand even though I did nothing.

Half an hour later, my phone pings, and my heart seizes when Alyssa's name flashes onto the screen.

your dog is the cutest

I bite my lip, but nothing can stop the smile from spreading across my face. I snap a picture of Smush, who's busy lying mournfully by his empty food bowl, and send it to her.

His life is quite tragic at the moment, so he appreciates your support

My phone starts vibrating, and I nearly drop it. Alyssa's responding to my text with a full-blown FaceTime call. I take a deep breath and run a hand through my stick-straight brown hair, doing nothing to fix the lack of volume, and accept the call.

"Please show me this sweet boy's face," Alyssa says as soon as her face fills my screen.

I hold my phone up to get a good angle, tilting it so that she can't see the massive pimple on my cheek.

"I don't know what you speak of, there are no sweet boys here. Only tiny demons who finished the last of my chocolate cake and had to be rushed to the pet hospital in the middle of the night."

That was a week ago, and Mom still brings it up every time Smush crosses her path.

Alyssa laughs, and my stomach tightens. It truly is the prettiest sound in the world.

"Show me this sweet boy with excellent taste in dessert."

I hop off the couch, crossing to the kitchen where Smush lies. He looks up at me hopefully, as though I'm here to share more of my cereal, but instead I switch the video so that Alyssa can get a full shot of his tragic expression.

"Hi, sweet boy," she coos. "I heard your mom doesn't want to share her chocolate with you."

I flip the camera back. "Hey. Whose side are you on here?"

"Oh, Smush's," she says immediately. "Always."

I shake my head at her. "Traitor."

She grins back at me, sparking the same warmth in my chest she always does in bio. But there, we're mandated by the Marinwood Public School District to hang out for forty-five minutes a day. Mr. Ray is there to fill lulls in the conversation with his lecturing. His nonsensical lab instructions are always there to fuel more conversations as we try to decipher how he wants us to handle the microscope.

Here, the brief lull feels like an endless silence. It's just us, on our phone screens, with nothing to distract from the fact that neither of us is talking. She fidgets on my screen for a moment, her bright eyes darting to the side. *Say something,* I plead with myself, but every thought that flashes through my brain feels horribly stupid, unbearably cringey.

If I stay on the call too long, she'll realize I'm not as funny as the TikTok video Eve made for me. My personality is about as great as my first attempt at a video, which is to say it should be deleted as quickly as possible before anyone sees that it only got four likes.

"I have to go," I say quickly. "I, um, I have to help my mom with dinner."

"Oh, yeah," Alyssa says. "Sorry, I didn't mean to call and disrupt your day. I—"

"No, no, I'm glad you got to see firsthand what a bad dog Smush is," I say, my shoulders curling inward as I say goodbye and hang up the call, awkwardness seeping out of my pores. I shudder as my screen goes dark. Why am I *like this?*

I pocket my phone and spin on my heel. "Eve!"

She bursts out of her bedroom, almost tripping down the stairs as she runs in her socks to me. "What's wrong? Oh god, did Smush eat the chocolate chips? I knew he'd figure out how to jump on the counter eventually. I'll call the poison control hotline, don't worry, it'll be fine, you get his travel bag so we can take him to the vet."

"No, no," I say, but I pick up the bag of chocolate chips and stow them safely back in the pantry. She has a point. "It's not him. Alyssa called."

She stares at me. "Good lord, Harp, the amount of pain in your voice. I thought at the very least, the house was on fire."

She drops into one of the stools that line the kitchen island, breathing hard. I grimace.

"Sorry. But my metaphorical house is burned to the ground."

She gives me a look that would be sympathetic if it didn't make it clear she was annoyed. "What happened?"

I slink onto the stool next to her, scooping up Smush on my way. He wriggles into a comfy position on my lap and goes back to his nap.

"She wanted to see Smush, and then I didn't know what to say."

Eve twists her hair into a braid as she squints at me. She got lucky, in that she got Mom's hair—blond and wavy and always shiny even though she barely uses conditioner half the time. "You could've said anything. If she called you, she obviously wants to talk to you."

"Only because she thinks I'm the mastermind of the Tik-Tok video," I say.

"Well, if she called you and you ended the conversation, the ball's in your court now," Eve says.

I grit my teeth. "No thank you, I don't want it."

Eve shakes her head at me with a teasing smile, but it drops off her face when she sees the puppy-dog eyes I'm making at her.

"No," she says before I can get the words out.

"Please," I say, widening my eyes as much as I can. I probably look more like a bug-eyed ogre than a puppy at this point, but I'm desperate. "You have to help me talk to her. Please. Pleasepleasepleasepleaseplease."

Eve gives a long-suffering sigh. "Give me your phone."

I give a whoop of victory and thumb the touchpad to unlock it before handing it over. Eve swipes to my texts and types quickly. She turns the phone back over to me and lets me read the message she's put together.

Smush wanted me to tell you that he thinks you're cute too, even if you did not bring him any snack offerings

I yelp and snatch the phone out of her hand before she can hit send.

"You can't *say* that," I screech as I delete the whole thing, careful not to send it by accident as I do.

Eve folds her arms. "Why not? It's fun and flirty. You have to put your feelings out there at some point."

"Because," I say, my face growing hot. "It's just too much. Tone it down."

Rolling her eyes, Eve takes the phone back. "I thought the point was to help you." But she dutifully types out another message, holding out the phone for my approval.

Smush is mad you didn't bring him any snacks.

I hit send, my stomach clenching as I do. At least there are no embarrassing references to how cute I think she is. Even if Eve did use Smush as a shield, there's no way I can just put myself out there like that. The thought of it makes me want to fold myself up into a dark corner where no one can see my red face.

Sadly that isn't possible, though, so I settle for ducking my head so Eve can't meet my eye.

"Tell me when she answers," Eve says as she saunters back to her room.

"She's typing," I yell after her before she reaches the stairs. "Where are you going?"

Eve pauses to give me a look, one foot on the stairs. "I have finals, Harp."

Panic shoots through my veins. I have no idea what Alyssa's about to say. What if she tells me she never wants to talk to me again? What if she tries to flirt?

I have no idea which one terrifies me more.

"Please," I say, my voice cracking.

Eve's lips are pursed so tight, I can barely see them as she makes her way back over to me. "What did she say?"

She leans across the kitchen island so that we're huddled together over my phone.

please tell him I'm very sorry

I bite my lip. "What can we do with that?"

Eve stares at me, sighing. "Well, if you'd actually flirt—"

"Absolutely not."

"Fine. Send her a picture of him with his dopey face, then."

I grimace as I type, but Eve nods approvingly as she reads over my shoulder. I breathe a sigh of relief as I hit send on the photo, a perfect joke to go along with it, and give Eve a grateful smile.

—

Every time I see the bouncing ellipsis that means Alyssa's typing, I run down the hall to Eve's room. She's working on her final project for one of her classes, a short film script, so she's up even when I kick down her door at 2:14 a.m.

She is not, however, happy to see me.

"Please go to bed."

I hand her my phone instead. She sighs, shaking her head at me as she takes it, scrolling through our chat history. We've spent the past hours talking about Alyssa's favorite sitcom, which Eve knew all about because she's writing a spec script episode of the show for one of her classes. I'm struggling to keep up with the conversation, since I've only watched a handful of episodes with Eve. I like it well enough, but I can't talk about it the way Eve can, the way she can get right to the heart of the story while making jokes so funny they could've been lifted right from the actors' mouths.

From there, we moved on to talking about our favorite

snack foods, where I barely needed Eve's help at all, and have now looped around to talking about TikTok again. I peer at our text chain over Eve's shoulder.

Your video was so clever

She responds instantly.

Thanks!! I was really nervous. Making jokes about it after helped a lot.

Eve meets my eye. "Just talk to her, Harp."

"I am," I protest. It's not my fault that hitting send makes my heartbeat throb in my fingertips and my head spin with nausea as the fear of sounding stupid floods my veins.

Eve types out a message and turns back to her work. I drop my gaze to my phone, and a horrible swooping feeling tears through my gut.

want to talk about it?

I've barely processed the words and their implication when my screen comes to life with a FaceTime call request from Alyssa. My throat seizes, and I hit Eve's shoulder.

She doesn't look up at me. "You better go back to your room and take that."

"I hate you," I huff before spinning on my heel and tearing down the hall.

I take a deep breath as I shut my bedroom door, but no amount of oxygen could calm my trembling insides. I arrange myself cross-legged on the bed. There's no way to get out of this, not now, not after what Eve said.

I hit accept.

"Hey," I say, forcing a smile when Alyssa's face fills my

screen. Too much. I look like an alien with a toothache. Tone it down.

"Hey," Alyssa says back. Her smile is perfectly normal. No, better than normal—it's like a piece of sunshine has lit up my room, even though it's the middle of the night. "It's nice to have someone to talk to at"—she pauses—"at two-thirty-one in the morning."

I laugh. "My new routine of waking up extremely late and funneling as much junk food into my mouth as I can does not lead to a normal bedtime."

It's all I can do not to close my eyes and shrivel under my bed frame as soon as the words leave my mouth. *Funneling junk food into my mouth* is not a cute image.

Alyssa laughs, though, which is nice of her.

"Same," she says. "Plus the three bottles of Coke I had at nine probably don't help."

"Three? You have a problem." I try to sound teasing, but I probably come off condescending.

She laughs again, though. "Oh, that was just after dinner. You should see my recycling bin. It's not pretty."

"Mr. Ray would be so disappointed in you," I say, thinking about the lab he made us do on soda and disintegration after we spent half a class period complaining about the school taking away the vending machines.

"Mr. Ray is wrong on that and many other counts," Alyssa says.

I raise my free hand in surrender. "Can't argue with that."

"Anyway, thanks for being so nice about the whole

me-coming-out thing," Alyssa goes on. "My parents have always been super understanding about things—"

"Yeah, they seemed like it on the video," I blurt before I can stop myself.

Alyssa grins. "Yeah. I can't believe they agreed to do that. But it was still scary, you know? Like, being vulnerable like that."

"Definitely," I say. "It was the same for me. I knew my parents would be supportive, but . . . I was so anxious the whole week leading up to when I decided to do it."

"When did you?" she asks.

I tell her the story, how I wanted to be cool and casual but ended up crying at the dinner table last year, confessing my crush on Madison Hartley. Mom thought the whole thing was hilarious, and she made a celebratory cake.

When I'm done, and grateful that the dimness of my room hides the redness of my cheeks (why did I have to tell her the bit about the crying?), Alyssa tells me how she convinced her parents to do the TikTok video by making them bribery banana bread. This inspires me to share a history of my baking fails, for some reason, and Alyssa laughs as I describe the time I almost set the kitchen on fire before trying to top it with her own story about coating the bottom of her oven in melted chocolate.

Eventually, she glances to the side, and gasps. "It's three-thirty in the morning."

My eyes widen. "Oh."

"I should probably get to sleep," she says. "But this was fun."

"Yeah," I say with a smile. *Yeah.* Real smooth, Harper.

As soon as she hangs up, I launch myself off my bed and burst back into Eve's bedroom. "How could you do that to me?"

Eve looks up from her laptop, her eyebrows raised so high they disappear into the fringe of her bangs. "Excuse me?"

"I embarrassed myself, like . . ." I pause, trying to count, but I quickly lose track of all the inane things that managed to come out of my mouth while I tried to flirt. "I don't even know how many times."

"Harp," Eve says, her voice gentle. "I'm sure that's not true. You're too hard on your—"

"I asked you to help," I say.

"And I said no," Eve says, the gentleness seeping out of her tone. "I have a final. In case you haven't noticed, Mom has been on my case since I've gotten home about my choice of major. And this final is actually really important for my career. The one no one in this family seems to care about. Not Mom, and certainly not you."

I shrink back, blinking fast at her. "Eve, I care ab—"

"If you did, you wouldn't be busting into my room every ten seconds while I'm trying to work because you don't know how to write a text. And maybe you'd stand up for me every once in a while when Mom starts going on and on about my choices."

I swallow thickly. "Eve, I . . . I'm sorry."

"Please," Eve says, turning away from me, "get out of my room so I can finish this."

I shut her bedroom door behind me, taking a deep breath in the dark hall before looking at my phone again. There's a text from Alyssa.

it was nice talking to you

How am I supposed to answer now? If Eve refuses to help me, Alyssa will notice the sudden drop in humor and the increase in painful awkwardness. And then texts from her will dry up.

I lock my phone and go to bed without answering.

—

When I wake up, at noon but still feeling groggy after a night of barely sleeping, I have another text waiting for me.

Okay you may be right about me having a problem.

Under it is a picture of her breakfast oatmeal, with a half-finished bottle of Coke next to it. I laugh, but the bubble of joy that I felt when I saw her name on my screen bursts when I remember that Eve won't help me anymore. What am I supposed to do now?

I leave my phone on my nightstand and head downstairs for a breakfast of my own. Or lunch, I suppose, at this point. I crack open a new box of Cinnamon Toast Crunch to fix myself a bowl—maybe I have a problem of my own—and eat it while staring into space. Every time I think about last night, I want to curl up into a tiny ball and disappear. And not just because of how cringey I was with Alyssa.

I've been pretty self-involved with Eve. This feels even worse than the time I cried at her thirteenth birthday because she chose a boring vanilla cake, and she made fun of me for years after that one. I have to make this right.

She must have stayed up even later than I did, because she's still asleep. As soon as I'm done eating my second bowl, which I top off a bit to finish the last of my milk—see? problem— I set about cleaning the kitchen. I clear off the island, then I set up the space with the sunflowers from the coffee table in the living room, a fancy pen I nab from Mom's office, and my favorite candle, which claims to smell like old books. I've just finished lighting it when Eve comes downstairs.

She stares at the kitchen, bleary-eyed. "Do you have a date or something?"

"No," I say, holding my arms out in a *ta-da!* motion. "I have an awesome older sister who needs a nicer workspace if she's ever going to finish her final."

Eve laughs. "You're cute."

"I'm sorry I bothered you all night," I say.

She wraps an arm around my shoulders. "It's fine. Being annoying is your job. I forgive you, but only if you promise to tell Mom how funny I am when she inevitably starts arguing with me tonight. I did make your whole relationship happen, so you can be the first official witness to my unending humor."

I hold out my pinkie, and she shakes it, like when we were little kids.

"You didn't make my whole relationship, though," I say. "That's definitely down the toilet."

Eve stares at me. "What did you do on the call?"

I summarize it for her, and she shakes her head at me. "You're the most ridiculous person I know."

"I know," I groan. "It's so embarrassing."

"No," Eve says with a laugh. "You're ridiculous because that's a perfectly normal and fun time you had. She clearly wants to talk to you again. Just be yourself, for the love of all that is holy, and leave me alone in my cute workspace because if I don't finish today I'm going to miss the deadline."

She spins on her heel to go to her room, and reemerges with her laptop and headphones, which she puts into her ears with a pointed look in my direction.

Taking the hint, I plop myself on the living room couch and try to let the hours disappear into a TikTok hole. Instead, I feel every agonizing second rip past. All I can think about is Alyssa's text, waiting for me. But every time I think about answering, the panicky shaking in my gut returns. What can I say to her?

It only gets worse when, a few hours later, she texts me again.

Is everything okay?

I bite my lip, hard. *No, everything is not okay, Alyssa,* I want to tell her. *Everything is in fact very bad. I like you so much, and the idea of saying the wrong thing to you makes me want to hide under a rock and never come out.*

Of course, I can't say that to her. Plus, now I have to give an explanation for why I ignored her text this morning.

I turn, about to call Eve, but she's busy writing. Instead, I think about what she told me yesterday. *You have to put yourself out there at some point.*

Isn't that what Alyssa and I talked about last night, about being vulnerable with people you care about?

I tap over to TikTok and hit record.

"Hi, guys," I say, waving at the camera. "I need you to help me make this go viral, because I majorly messed things up with my crush and I have to fix it."

The rest of the video is a montage of me packing all the Coke cans I can fit into a cardboard box, along with a pack of chocolate chips, because why not? And the scariest part: the note. I don't show the video what it says. That's just for Alyssa.

I'm so sorry I didn't answer earlier!! To be totally and probably cringily honest, I was scared. Like we were saying last night, being vulnerable with someone you care about is scary. And I have a whole lot of anxiety, so that doesn't help. But anyway, the point is, I like you. Even though you have a massive problem with carbonated beverages

"Next step, ride this over to her house," I say to the camera, filming myself as I clip my bike helmet on. I balance my phone on top of the package in my handlebar basket to edit together quick cuts of me biking the twenty minutes to Alyssa's place, dropping the package off on her front porch, and hurrying off with my fingers crossed.

When we get back home, I post the video and text Alyssa.

The typing bubble appears almost immediately. And hovers at the bottom of my screen for what feels like a hundred lifetimes. I can see myself growing old as she composes her message, taking her sweet time.

Eventually, her response pops up.

I like you too

Even though you do not understand the power/access that Coke has

Also your video is great but you really shouldn't TikTok and bike

I bite back a laugh as I check my profile. TikTok has done me a solid here—the video has done just as well as Eve's Smush masterpiece.

"Eve," I call out.

She takes out a headphone. "I swear on that typewriter I got for my birthday, if you say one more word I will take you out with the trash."

"I told Alyssa I like her," I say quickly, before she can put her headphone back in.

She rips out the other one to run over and give me a hug. "Never thought I'd see the day."

"Thank you for your faith in me," I respond dryly.

She pats my head, and I slap her hand as she goes back to her workspace. I turn back to my phone, the panicky feeling fizzing away as I text Alyssa.

The New Boy Next Door

by Natasha Preston

They've been living here for two weeks and four days.

Lockdown began two weeks ago.

Our next-door neighbor, Mr. Cotton, was telling Mom that the Brady family brought COVID-19 here. As if they packed it in their boxes. He's the neighborhood gossip, heavily into conspiracy theories. I wouldn't be surprised to learn he's converted his basement into a doomsday bunker.

I look out my window and can just about see Archer Brady lounging on a sunbed in his backyard, staring at his cell. He looks around my age. Tall, dark hair, square jaw, high cheekbones that Michelangelo himself couldn't have sculpted any better. Archer belongs on a teen drama series, starring as the angry one who eventually wins everyone over.

So far, he hasn't won anyone over

Except me, that is. I can't seem to make myself stop watching. He's one of those people you can't help staring at as you try to figure out how it's fair they look so perfect.

The fact that his house is right next to mine doesn't help the growing obsession.

So far we've seen each other when our moms have come back from the grocery store and we've been outside helping take things from the car. Twice that has happened and all we've done is raise our hand in a little wave. It still sends my heart on a sprint. I haven't heard his voice, but I've wondered so many times if he wants to talk, to make a friend. To sit in my tree and chat.

Between our houses is an old gnarly tree that looks dead in the winter but is full of lush green leaves in the spring. It's so big that not even my dad and mom can get their arms around it together; it takes the three of us to be able to reach. Only our backyards are fenced, so we have shared access to the tree at the side of each other's houses.

I used to climb it with Sabi. She's my best friend, and her family lived in the house before the Bradys moved in. Sabi and I would chill in the tree for hours. It's where she told me about her crush on Hunter, football star, and I told her about my first kiss with Hunter's older brother, Roman.

Archer throws one leg over the other, crossed at the ankles on the sun lounger . . . that's in the shade! If he's going to stay in the shade, he might as well be inside. They have a pool, but I haven't seen him use it yet. Good thing, really. I'll probably pass out if I see him shirtless.

I bite my lip as he runs his hand through his messy black hair.

I have only spoken to his mom. I don't know where his dad is.

His head raises almost directly at me as if he can sense I'm spying. My breath catches. Jumping back, I spin around and flatten my back against the wall.

Damn it! If he saw me, he will definitely think the girl next door is a total creep. All we've done is catch each other's eye in the window or outside.

Maybe he didn't actually see from that far away.

"Quinn! Shouldn't you be online? You have school, right?"

My least favorite words to hear from my mom. School at home. There is no God. But she's right. It's almost time for class.

I trudge downstairs like I'm off to war.

I find Mom in the kitchen. My laptop is open and water bottle filled. Both sit neatly on the table. She's prepped my classroom.

"You don't have to do this," I tell her as I sit my butt at the table and smile up at her. "It's not like I'm going to forget."

We're on day fifteen of being at home. Day fifteen of missing Taco Bell, Starbucks Frappuccinos, and hanging with friends. Day fifteen of one walk a day. Mom stops to gossip with the neighbors who are in their front yard. I just keep thinking about everything I'm missing.

Social distancing is weird. But one bright spot: every house on our block has a chalkboard in their yard. We leave messages and encouragement. I love reading them on our walks. On ours, Mom has written: *This too shall pass.* One of my favorites has been *2021 will be our year.*

Archer's is still blank.

The conversation with everyone is the same most days. Lots of talk about "crazy times," "the damn virus," and "living like prisoners." I don't think prisoners can order food in, hang out in the sun, and swim in pools they have in their own backyard, but sure.

"Hey, Mom?"

She turns from where she's chopping apples. That better be for a pie.

"Yeah?"

"When you met Archer and his mom . . . did he say much?"

"He grunted a hello and went inside. Bit rude, if you ask me. Though I suppose we don't know their circumstance for moving here. No friends or family here, no dad around. Not that I've seen, anyway. Now, finish your work."

I put my head down and focus. Hours pass. The smell of warm apple pie wafts through the kitchen.

And the very second I announce that I'm finished, Mom thrusts my Vans in my face.

"Let's get out for a bit," she says.

Our walk is the highlight of her day. I slip my Vans on and follow her to the front door.

"What's that?" I ask, eyeing the covered plate she's holding in her hands.

"Apple pie for Mrs. Langford down the road. She's missing

her grandchildren. We've got to look after each other now more than ever."

So she made my favorite pie and it's not for me.

Of course I notice him the second I step out of the front door. Somewhere inside me is an Archer Brady radar. Archer is taking out the trash—that seems to be his job—and he's doing it while scowling at the whole world.

And oh my god. He's much closer to me than he's ever been. My stomach clenches like it's independently working on some abs. His eyes follow me.

I'm pretty sure my brain is short-circuiting right now. I hope he doesn't speak because I don't think I can.

Everything about him is angry: the narrowed eyes, clenched jaw, and tight shoulders.

It should be illegal that he looks so good while doing it.

I wipe my damp palms on my shorts.

Stop staring.

I'm mostly a happy person, I like to smile, I like having fun and laughing, so why am I so drawn to him? It doesn't make sense, but I want to know everything. I want to dig into his brain and learn every part of his life, the good and the bad. And I want to run my fingers all over that magnificent face and through that inky hair.

Calm down, Quinn.

Now is not the time to develop a new crush. Especially on someone who is more likely to push me over during my morning yoga than join in.

"Hello," Mom says, waving at him.

I stop breathing. *Is she crazy?* She's talking to him!

Don't trip over.

He jerks his chin in some sort of greeting. It screams *I can't be bothered with you.* I don't imagine he would be massively concerned about insulting people, so I suppose we should take the nod.

Wow. Okay, I thought his eyes were brown, but up this close I can see that they're dark blue, like the midnight sky. They linger like he's trying to commit my face to memory so he can draw me later.

All we have done is stare at each other for slightly too long. Every conversation we've had over two weeks has been silent and spoken exclusively with our eyes. I feel like I know him without actually knowing him. It's the oddest feeling and I can't explain it. Right now, all it would take is six steps. Six of my little steps and I would be right in front of him.

His mouth parts and I think he's going to talk to me. That happens a lot, he opens his mouth or goes to take another step, then retreats with nothing. I want to talk to him so bad, but I'm terrified of the way he makes me feel, so I just walk away.

It's not normal to be this invested in a person you haven't even said one word to.

My heart misses a beat when he takes one last look—his face turned down, almost sad—over his shoulder before walking around the side of his house.

—

"Quinn?" Mom says.

I jolt as she places her hand on my arm. "What?"

"Are you okay?" Her face is full of amusement.

"Fine."

"I think . . . I think he's climbing up in the tree," she says, straining to see between our houses now that we're past his.

"Huh?"

"Archer. He's in the tree."

My and Sabi's tree. I look up and see him on her branch, legs kicked out, leaning back against the trunk. My branch runs at a ninety-degree angle to his and just a smidge lower down.

"Go and talk to him." She takes the pie from me. "I'll deliver this."

"But you wanted to walk."

"I can still walk. *You* wanted to know what his story is, so go and find out. Looks like he could use a friend right now."

I bite my lip as I weigh up my options. Walk around the neighborhood having the same conversation at every house from the sidewalk . . . or go and grill Mr. Happy.

"We're all in this together, the whole street, remember? Go, Quinn," she says with a laugh and a nudge.

"Okay. Tell me what the signs say today."

"I will. Keep your distance up there."

"I know, I know."

"No touching," she says with a wicked smile.

I give her a look close to the one I gave Dad when he accidentally broke my favorite *Twilight* coffee mug.

There is no danger of me touching him, even if there were no virus. I can't even look at him without getting flustered.

He might tell me to get lost, but he has no right to. The tree is right in the middle of our properties and no one seems to know who it belongs to.

Can I really do this? I have to. There's no choice. We can't spend the rest of our lives here not talking but desperately wanting to.

Time to be brave, Quinn Reeve.

I walk over to the tree, reach up, grab the next branch, and push myself up. My heart flutters as I feel his eyes on me the whole time, waiting for me to get to the top. I shuffle back on the branch that's about as wide as my waist and smile.

He doesn't kick me out of the tree, so I figure he doesn't mind company. I'm going to pretend that he wants me to come up here.

Wow, he's even prettier this close.

He stares off into space, flicking a large coin between his fingers. I can't see which one it is, but it's not something I would have thought he'd own.

"Hi," I say, licking my dry lips.

He blinks and slides the coin into his pocket, then pulls the little bud out of his ear. He watches me with curiosity. I can't tell what he's thinking because he has an awesome poker face.

"What are you listening to?" I ask.

Oh my god, I can't believe I'm actually talking to him!

He's wearing a black Foo Fighters T-shirt. "Music," he replies, sounding bored and inconvenienced.

All right, I totally believe that he was being rude when Mom first met him.

If that's how we're going to play it, fine. "You look like an Ariana fan to me."

Except that he looks like he's into angry, shouty music, and sacrificing kittens.

His eyebrow lifts. *Ooh, we have a reaction.*

"Ariana?"

Oh, the voice. Deep and a little rough like he's woken up before he was ready. It's my new favorite sound.

"I'm not here to judge. I like the Killers and Fall Out Boy myself."

"What's your name?" he asks, sitting up straight and removing the other bud. Did Mom not tell them my name? Or did he not listen?

Now I have his full attention and it half makes me want to run away and hide. Can you sweat from your eyeballs?

The sun shines on one side of his face and makes it look like he has chocolate highlights—same shade as me—in his black hair. I doubt he's dyed it, though.

"I'm Quinn."

"How old are you?" he asks.

The way he looks at me makes me squirm. "Seventeen. You?"

His mouth thins like he's irritated at the thought of being questioned. I hold my ground. I'm not saying anything else until he does.

It's a battle of wills, and I'm not going to lose.

Finally, his shoulders sink. "Seventeen."

I win.

"I just turned seventeen," I add. "My birthday was May fifth."

"Eighteen in October."

I don't get to know *when* in October he turns eighteen, then.

"Do you think we'll still be in lockdown for your birthday?" I ask.

"I couldn't care less."

I wave my hand. "Doesn't matter if we are, I'll throw you a tree party."

His lip quirks, about to grin and give him up. The dude might act like everyone is a nuisance to him, but he's enjoying our conversation as much as I am.

"A tree party?"

"Yes, with streamers and balloons and cake! I'll sing. I was in glee club in middle school."

There is no stopping this smile from coming. He shows pearly white teeth and shakes his head. "Glee club?"

"Uh-huh. It was fun for a year, but I didn't want to do it in high school."

"Because you would get your head flushed?"

I cross my arms, but I'm not at all offended. "Well, that's not nice, is it? I wonder what clubs you have been in." He opens his mouth, but I steamroll ahead. "No, let me guess. Now, I'm thinking you've never been in one because it's 'uncool.'" I actually use air quotes. "But you've desperately wanted to be in the debate club, put all that moody, argumentative energy to good use."

He doesn't blink, doesn't move, and I'm not sure he breathes either.

I'd call vampire if it weren't bright out.

"Oh, no, I got it!" I snap my fingers. "Ariana appreciation club. Foo Fighters are an awesome band, by the way." The intense way he watches me has my cheeks burning. The words won't stop coming.

"Do you drink coffee?" he asks.

"Yeah, why?"

"Stop. You don't need the caffeine."

"You spend a lot of time on your phone."

"You seem to spend a lot of time watching me."

Busted. It's not all one-sided, though. "There's not a lot else to do."

He straightens his legs, leaning one over the other on the branch. It's a dangerous move, I almost fell once doing the same.

"You should be careful," I say.

"I'm not going to fall." He turns back so I can see his profile again.

I shrug, smiling and turning away. "Don't listen, it'll be amusing for me."

"Why did you come up here?" he asks. His low voice is the first hint of vulnerability.

"I haven't been in this tree since Sabi."

"None of what you just said makes sense."

I pick at a lump of bark that's lifting from the branch. "Sabi was my best friend, her family lived in your house. We used to meet up here all the time."

He nods. "You hate me being here."

I shake my head but he's still not facing me. "I don't."

"You got up here pretty quick when you saw me. I thought I was getting an eviction notice. Whose tree is it?"

"No one knows. I don't mind you being up here. I kinda felt sad for the tree the last five months, having no one sitting in it."

Now he looks. Slowly, his head turns to me. "You felt sad for the *tree*?"

"Let's move straight past that one and leave it at you being welcome."

"At least I'm welcome somewhere. This neighborhood is weird. The chalkboard messages are weird."

"The chalkboards are amazing; it keeps us close when we have to be apart. The people won't always be weird. Well, they will, but they'll love you guys in no time. Everyone looks after each other. We have street parties and parades and you'll get lots of baked treats. Not even for any reason. They just need to get to know you. It's all a bit crazy right now because there's a lot of fear."

"Of me and my mom?"

"Um, no, the whole pandemic thing. You should come out on your front yard tomorrow evening, after six."

"Why?"

"Home street party."

His reaction is silence like he's trying to figure out if I'm joking or not. "A *home* street party?"

"Yeah, we're all decorating our houses and cooking in our front yards. The Ebson brothers who live across from you are playing live music. You and your mom should join in."

Our drives are opposite sides of the house so there is just grass—and a tree—between us. We could sit on the lawn near each other. I just want to keep talking to him.

He shakes his head. "I don't want anyone in my business."

"So don't tell them the things you don't want them to know."

And, wow, do I want him to tell me now.

"Do you wish you'd moved somewhere else? Or not moved at all?" I ask.

His eyes lift from the floor and delve into mine. My heart skips. "No, I don't think I do."

I smile, though I'm feeling myself getting a little hysterical at the way he looks at me. The fluttering in my stomach can be more closely compared to a stampede.

"Good." I clear my throat. "You're going to love it here. Are you starting school in August? Mom doesn't think we'll go back before. This summer is going to be the longest ever."

I'm suddenly not too unhappy about that. I might not be able to see my friends for a while, but I can see Archer.

"Senior year. Can't wait." His voice is laced with sarcasm.

"Of course. You don't like school either. What *do* you like?"

"Music."

"Do you play?"

"Guitar."

"That's awesome. I wanted to learn guitar."

"What stopped you?"

"I really suck."

He chuckles and the sound makes me smile. I made him laugh! I thawed his icy heart, cracked the tough exterior. I rock.

"Archer?"

We both look back at his house. His mom is calling him from somewhere inside.

I find her at his window. When she looks across and sees me with him, she smiles.

She slides the window up. "Hello, Quinn."

I wave. "Hi, Mrs. Brady." So Mom *did* tell them my name.

"Call me Juliet."

Well, that's a good sign. I wasn't sure if she was going to tell him to come in and get away from me. We're a safe distance from each other.

"Archer, lunch is ready."

He nods at her and turns to me. "I'll see you later, Ace."

Ace?

He climbs down two branches, then jumps, landing on his feet the way my nan's dog jumps fences.

I was off with vampire. Werewolf?

"Juliet?" I say.

She keeps her hand on the window but doesn't shut it. "Yes?"

"Have you heard about the street party tomorrow? Everyone stays in their own front yard. We're all putting lights up and eating outside."

She smiles. "Yes, I did hear."

"It would be cool if you and Archer could come out, too."

With a smile, she replies, "I think we might. See you later, Quinn."

I wave again and swivel around, leaning my back against the enormous trunk of the tree.

Being in the tree again feels good. I thought it would be weird. I've avoided it for months, but the second my hand touched that branch to climb, I felt happy.

And we spoke. Finally!

Damn, that boy is built to break hearts. I wonder what he was like at his old school. Did he have lots of girlfriends? Did he refuse to let anyone close? That wouldn't surprise me.

God, I'm in trouble.

I grip the branch and climb down, placing every step without looking. I bet I could get up and down this tree blindfolded.

I get down and shake my head. Two weeks into lockdown and I'm obsessing over the new boy next door. Full-on obsessed now that we've spoken. Archer is more than a bad attitude.

He called me *Ace*. That's going to drive me crazy until I figure out why.

I'm practically gliding as I walk into the house. We had a conversation. He said single words at first, but then he formed sentences. I've been watching him out of my window for weeks and now I've officially met him. I don't want to get ahead of myself and say we're going to have a beautiful friendship, but we sat in my happy tree and that has to be good luck.

I want to jump up and down and do a little spin. My cheeks ache with the goofy smile he's put on my face.

Kicking my shoes off, I head upstairs to read. I grab my paperback and sit on the seat beneath the window that my dad built. He made it because I love to sit and watch the rain . . . and Archer apparently.

We're on talking terms now; it's extra creepy to watch a friend. Or an almost-friend.

I've purposefully sat with my side against the window, facing the wrong way. Gone are my days of stealing glances of the mysterious Archer Brady. All eighteen days of them, poof, gone. I will be normal from here on out and wait until we meet in our tree.

I can absolutely do normal.

Opening the book, I remove my bookmark—there's a special place reserved in hell for people who fold the pages—and continue where I left off.

Someone is about to die. The stalker is in the house.

I wonder if he's in the backyard.

If this character falls down the stairs as she flees, I'm giving up.

Tap, tap, tap.

I lower the book. That wasn't in my head.

Tap, tap, tap.

Sticking the bookmark back between the pages, I put the book down and look out the window.

My eyes swing to Archer's window. He's there. But what is that? I lean closer and almost bump my face on the glass.

Scribbled in red are numbers on his window.

He moves back in front of the window, eyes meeting mine, and taps once more on the glass. Then he walks off.

His cell number. That must have taken ages, he had to write the numbers backward.

Leaping off my seat, I dash to my bed to grab my cell. My heart is flying as I type the number in. I'm not even going to overthink this. I'm texting him right now. I'll be cool and casual. He wouldn't have given me his number two minutes after our first conversation if he didn't want me to message him.

Chewing on my lip, I send a text and press the cell into my fluttering tummy.

Quinn: I hope you didn't use a Sharpie.

The phone beeps and I jump so high that I almost launch it. Instant response. I open the message and a high-pitched squeal leaves my throat. *Pitiful, Quinn.*

Archer: It's my blood.

I roll my eyes, my smile wide and moronic.

Quinn: Wouldn't surprise me. Do you give your number to all of the neighbors that way?

Archer: No. I gave it to Jayde via carrier pigeon.

Jayde lives in the house on the other side of Archer. She's a senior and even less of a people person than Archer. They would make good friends.

Quinn: You two would get along very well.

Typing the words makes my top lip curl. *Calm down, you don't own him.* I don't even know him and I'm jealous. That's just great. Lockdown wasn't supposed to send me crazy. I was going to sunbathe, swim, and read. I was supposed to come out of this with a swimmer's body, Mensa mind, and golden tan. Instead I'm going to be green, with a mushy brain, and a Jell-O body.

Archer: We had a whole two-minute conversation with about three words. I'm not her people.

At least with me there is conversation. When I'm nervous, I talk, and Archer sure brings out the nerves.

Quinn: Who are your people? What was that coin you had in the tree?

Archer: My grandpa's 20-year military challenge coin. He left it to me.

Quinn: That's sweet that he wanted you to have it.

I wait. And wait. And obsess. He didn't answer the question about who his people are. I'm obviously wanting him to say me. *Take the hint, Brady!*

How many minutes have passed since his last message? One? Two? A million?

I tap my leg while my phone does nothing at all. He's not going to reply.

That's fine. I have better things to do, too.

I put my phone down and head to find Mom. We make dinner together, eat with Dad, who tells us about his uneventful day.

It's hard, but I don't check my phone until I go to bed.

There is a message from him, sent ten minutes ago. I take a breath before I open it.

Archer: Night

Quinn: Night

We're at the saying good night stage. I want to jump around my room, but my parents will hear. Dad will threaten Archer with bodily harm if he hurts me.

In the morning, I shower, get dressed, and give Dad a hug as he heads out to work at the fire station. Today we're prepping for the home street party. I bound into the kitchen with a light heart, buzzing with energy.

Mom laughs. "It's good to see that smile back."

"I'm happy." My heart is on a constant rhythm that beats *Arch-er.*

"I can tell. It makes me happy, too. I'm prepping the food. Can you put the lights up and write on the chalkboard?"

"Totally."

Dad has hooks around the door and first-floor windows so it's super easy to hook the lights on. I grab the box of colored lights and chalk sitting by the front door ready and take them out.

I put the box on the doorstep and take the chalk to the board. Before I get there, though, I hear his voice.

"Mornin', Ace."

I take a breath and look over my shoulder. He's standing by his own chalkboard. The one he found ridiculous. I can just imagine his face as Mr. Cotton dropped it off.

"You're getting on board with the chalk." If I sound smug it's because I am.

He shrugs as if it's no big deal. We both know that's not true. It means maybe that he's settling in, maybe even enjoying it here.

"What's that?" I ask, walking across my yard. I stop short of the boundary. It's weird acting as if everyone is infectious.

He stands away from whatever is poking out of the ground. It's a ball of twinkle lights on a stick. There are more of them lying on the ground. As he spots me staring, his lips curve into the cutest smile ever.

My stomach flutters. *Welcome back, butterflies.*

"You're coming to the street party?" I ask, trying to ignore the light-headed feeling I get when he looks at me. I really hope I didn't sound too excited.

"I guess we are. Mom has ingredients everywhere ready to make . . . I don't know what she's making, but I'm sure we won't be able to eat it all."

"Mine is the same. She's also making you guys something."

He chuckles and walks over, leaving his lights behind. Kind of the way I have. We're drawn together. The lights can wait.

"Everyone on this street is a feeder."

"Correct," I confirm. "But they're all good cooks so be prepared for the most awesome food coma of your life. Seriously, if Mrs. Langford offers you brownies, take them. I could live off them alone. And the sugar cookies from—"

"Quinn," he says, cutting me off and lifting his dark eyebrow. "Did you have coffee?"

I shake my head. "No."

It's not caffeine that makes me hyper. It's him.

Twiddling my fingers behind my back, I smile. I hate people who can be so casual around their crush. I've never felt nervous around a guy before. Not like this anyway.

"I'm decorating," I say.

That could have gone better. I could have talked about bands, TV shows, school, literally *anything* else. But no, I state the damn obvious.

I smile wider and he smirks as if he can read my mind. "I can see that," he says.

I did so well in the tree, what is happening now? My mind is blank. Nothing but tumbleweed here.

"You okay, Ace?"

The humor in his voice makes me wish I were holding something I could throw it at him.

"I'm fine. Did you get the ink off your window?"

"Yeah. Don't want anyone else calling me."

He wants me to *call* him? I can only be cool on text.

"You should get back to your lights, I'll see you tonight," he says.

I nod but I'm disappointed to cut this short.

He chuckles as he walks away.

Okay, you're fine. I go back to my lights and force myself to focus. I will not look at him again until tonight. I'm too obvious and he's loving it. He was the one to give me his number, though.

Tonight, I get to spend hours with him and his mom. I want my parents to get along with them, too.

Mission one: make the whole street a happy family.

Mission two: get the lights up.

Mission three: act cool around Archer.

Not in order.

I look up as I'm about to turn and my mouth parts.

Written on his chalkboard is one word: *Ace.*

Well, I'm not going to be able to focus on other things I need to do now, am I?

The rest of the day drags, obviously. We get set up, prep the food, and then I swim in our pool. I read my old ratty copy of *Twilight* because I need the solidarity Bella offers with her instant Edward obsession.

By 5:58, I'm losing my mind and clock watching.

Mom and Dad are highly amused, teasing me about Archer, but mostly they're happy that I "have my spark back."

Why the hell does he call me Ace?

"I think we can go out now, Quinn," Dad says, waggling his eyebrows. "I can't wait to spend time with our new neighbors."

My eyes widen. "Do not say anything!"

Laughing, he pretends to zip his mouth and heads out the front door.

He better mean that.

I help Mom take food out and flick the twinkle lights on as we go.

Everyone is outside. Lights flicker up and down the street and the Ebson brothers strum the first chord on the makeshift stage they've set up. Music drifts through the street. The evening is warm, and the scent of barbecuing food fills the air. I take a breath and smile.

Mom walks up to the edge of our property to speak to Juliet. Archer is standing with a drink, red Solo cup to his mouth, eyes pinned on me.

My steps almost falter but I manage to make myself walk to the edge of our grass. I'm far enough away from Mom and Juliet that they won't be eavesdropping. Archer meets me, stopping about ten feet away. Beside us is our tree.

He has this gravitational pull and it takes real effort to not walk closer.

"People have gone all out," he says.

"Awesome, isn't it. This is what it's like all the time. Best street in the world."

His smile is sarcastic as if he's trying to disagree.

Neighbors stop by like we have been given shifts, everyone saying hello while keeping a safe distance back. Food is dropped in little brown parcels, some with a small hand sanitizer taped to the side.

We watch the Ebsons play. Their sign has two drawings of guitars and reads: *Rock off, COVID.* I've read a couple others that I can see from here. *Apocalyptic party 2020. United We Stand. You're all my heroes.*

Archer's is my favorite. *Ace.* I'm *desperate* to know.

The sun is setting, making the twinkle lights grow brighter. I'm sitting on a picnic blanket on the ground. Archer is doing the same from his yard.

"See how awesome it is here," I say, soaking in the atmosphere. "*And* you get to see me every day."

He pretends to look horrified as he takes a bite of a Hershey bar that Mr. Cotton dropped off like a peace offering. I guess he's decided they're okay now. I'm sure he'll have a new conspiracy soon about something else.

Missions one, two, and three are complete. Though I'm not sure how successful I've been staying cool in his presence, but he hasn't run away so I'm calling it a win.

"The town has its good points."

"When lockdown is lifted, I'll take you to the best places. We'll go bowling, trampolining—"

"Trampolining?"

I wave my hand. "You'll love it. There's also an awesome music store, lots of instruments and old vinyls."

He rests his arms on his knees. "I want to hear how bad you are at guitar."

"Your ears will bleed."

"I'll take my chances. I'll teach you."

"I'm totally up for that." The words leave my mouth far too quickly. *Abort mission 'Be Cool,' it's never gonna happen.*

He laughs. "I thought you would be."

"We could start a band," I joke. "Who will sing?"

"I used to sing."

"And play the guitar?"

"I can walk and talk at the same time, too," he says sarcastically.

"Oh my god, you're hilarious."

He rolls his eyes and smiles.

"What happened to your old band?"

Shrugging, he replies, "I moved away."

"You can start a new one."

"With you?"

"No, not really. I do suck. I'll be up front cheering."

"Hmm, I've always liked the idea of having a groupie."

"Let's not get ahead of ourselves. You might not be that good yet."

I could listen to him laugh all day.

"What's the first thing you're going to do when restrictions are lifted?" I ask.

"Drive around town with my tour guide."

"Right. Trampoline park."

He raises an eyebrow as if I've suggested we do each other's makeup.

"Our first date isn't going to be at a trampoline park."

Oh. A date. A *date*.

Off you pop, COVID. I've got a date with Archer, and I can't wait!

The Ebsons begin their second set, playing "All About You."

I glance over just as Archer's gaze falls to my lips. Curling my fingers into my palms, I take a breath and count back from ten. *You are not going to jump over there. You are not going to even acknowledge the fact that he wants to kiss you.*

We're not allowed to get kissing close.

But one day we will.

—

About six hours later, I sit with my back against the tree and look up. The sky is the color of Archer's eyes. The party is over, my parents are inside watching a movie, but I'm too restless to sleep.

I'm not surprised when I hear him climb the tree. The surprise is that he has a rucksack on his back.

He sits on his branch, and I look up to see his profile. Then he turns his head and the intensity in his face almost knocks me out of the tree.

"Hey," he says, raking his hand through his dark hair.

"You went inside an hour ago. Are you sleepwalking? I'm not carrying you downstairs and putting you back to bed."

Whatever he was expecting me to say, it wasn't that. His lips press tightly together as he fails to suppress his amusement. His eyes give him away, they're doing the smiling.

"I'm fine, thanks, Quinn. How are you?"

I laugh and shake my head.

"*Are* you okay?" he asks.

"I'm fine. I like my tree."

I vowed to never come up here again but thanks to him, it's my happy place again. It's calming. He's given me that gift and it feels amazing.

He nods. "The tree is . . ."

"Perfect."

"Let's not go that far."

"You're acting chill, but you love the tree and you like it here. You never say much, not about how you feel anyway. I dare you to admit it."

His eyes light up. "You dare me? Are we seven?"

"Chicken."

He blinks heavily.

"Yes, I called you a chicken."

I'm either talking so fast and so much that he can't keep up or talking absolute crap. I need to find a saner middle ground.

"I'm not falling for that, Ace."

"Do you like living here? I think you do; you've been smiling the last couple of days. It's the first time I've seen it."

"Just how much have you been stalking me?"

"Observing," I correct. Anyone have a fan for my face? It's on fire.

He rolls his eyes. "Sure. I don't hate it here."

"That's about as good as I'm going to get, isn't it? I thought things went well tonight. We had a good time, right? I mean we talked a lot and ate a lot. Everyone had fun."

His lips part. "Is your head the same as your mouth?"

"Excuse me?"

"When you're thinking, is your brain going nonstop?"

"Oh. Yeah, it's pretty much like a constant tornado of thoughts in my head."

"Do you ever have bad days? I have this theory that you're some sort of robot. Like a government experiment to put one in the community and see if anyone notices."

"If that were true, I'd go back, get a software update, and finish school now."

He laughs again.

"You know, I've thought that you are either a vampire or a werewolf."

"What do you think now? Oh, and I totally had you pegged as a *Twilight* fan."

"Team Edward all the way, baby. Now I think you're all right."

"I'm all right. Try not to inflate the ego too much, Quinn."

I laugh. "Do you still think I'm a robot?"

He takes the coin out of his pocket and passes it from finger to finger. "No. Now I think you're the most incredible person I've ever met."

He couldn't have surprised me more if he pushed me out of the tree.

A laugh rumbles through the tree. "Wow, that's how you silence Quinn Reeve."

I'm surprised my mouth isn't hanging open.

Words exist. Why can't I think of a single one?

Tilting his head back, he laughs and grips the coin in his palm like he's scared he'll drop it. "I think I like your shocked face the most."

I snap my teeth together. I'm incredible and he likes my face.

Taking a breath to compose myself—it doesn't work—I sit up straighter.

"My best face is my shocked one?" I rasp. My stupid voice is wobbly, making me sound like an absolute idiot.

"All right, you got me. Your smile is better. The best, actually."

"Have *you* had coffee?" I ask. What is going on here?

I'm rewarded with yet another laugh. "No, but I might be tired of pretending that I don't want to be around you all the time. Every day for the past two weeks, I've seen you smiling and trying to make everyone else smile. I can't stop looking out for you whenever I pass a window, you're like some sort of human magnet. I've been so intrigued by you. And so desperate to talk to you, it's embarrassing. I've caught you watching me more times than you'd admit."

"Confession time is my favorite," I mutter.

He gives me a flat look. "That's because so far I'm doing

all the confessing. But that's fine, you came and spoke to me first."

"Why didn't you?"

He shrugs. "You're . . . much more than anything I've experienced. It was a little scary to want the girl next door so bad when you've never spoken to her." He winces as though the confession is actually hurting him. "I really like you, Quinn. And I like all of your faces. They're all beautiful."

My heart thuds in my chest so fast I'm seeing stars. It's the best feeling in the world, kind of like flying without lifting an inch off the floor. My fingers curl into the bark. All I want to do is climb closer.

"I like you too, Archer."

His chin dips in a nod and his smile widens. "Yeah, I know. You're not subtle."

Oh, great. "I don't even know how you get eyes that color. It's insane and unfair."

When he looks at me, I almost melt into a puddle. Those. Damn. Eyes.

"Hold this for me a sec," he says, flicking something at me.

My eyes bulge; I lift my hands and snap them together. I caught it. Opening my palms, I see his coin. "Archer?"

"It's a test. No one has held that since my grandpa gave it to me. I punched a kid at my last school for trying to take it. It doesn't feel wrong handing it to you. Keep it safe for now."

I curl my hand shut and hold it against my racing heart. He's trusting me with his grandpa's coin.

"What are you doing?" I ask.

"Be patient."

I can't. I'm slowly going crazy, wondering what you're up to with that bag.

"Do you have supplies? Are we running away?" I ask.

He smirks, taking out his iPad. It's in a case with a handle. Attached to the handle is a loop of string.

This is getting a bit weird.

"Archer?"

"Patience, Ace."

"Why do you call me that? It was on your chalkboard." Today ours read: *No virus will keep us down.*

His eyes flit to me. "I'm not confessing that one yet."

"Unfair."

While hanging the iPad off two small broken branches so it faces us and doesn't swing, he glances my way. "You tell me how long you've been watching me for, and I'll tell you what it means. It was day one for me."

Well, there's no point in pretending now, not when he's admitting the same. "Since the day you moved in. I thought people who look like you were only on TV."

He nods. "Ace is ranked the highest in a deck of cards."

My mouth pops open audibly.

I'm his ace?

"You've gone silent again."

"Uh-huh," I mutter like a fool.

"Seriously, confession time is very one-sided."

"I'm obsessed with you. Are we even now?"

His smile does stupid things to me. "We're even."

"Good."

He taps the screen and brings up *Twilight* on Amazon Video.

"Get comfortable," he says.

Wait, we're not talking more about this ace thing?

"Twilight?" I ask.

He grunts, and I have no doubt that this isn't his first choice. Or his hundredth.

Digging in his bag, he balances a can of Coke and a bag of Haribo on a branch between us. Then puts the same on his lap. He hangs the bag on another branch and sits back.

Bella's voice floats from the iPad.

"We're watching a movie," I say, smiling while my heart does its racing *Arch-er* beat.

His eyes connect with mine. "No, Ace, we're having our first date."

Love with a Side of Fortune

by Jennifer Yen

"I'm sorry to tell you this, mèimei, but this is not your year."

Auntie Xin tsks as she glances down at the weathered pages of her trusted notebook. Wearing a pastel pink tracksuit and framed by a generic picture of a field hanging crookedly on the wall behind her, she looks like anything but the world-renowned fortune-teller she claims to be. Even the grainy photographs of her with vaguely familiar "celebrities" does little to distract from the fact that we're crammed into the back office of her Asian snack shop in Houston's Chinatown.

For as long as I can remember, Mom has been one of Auntie Xin's most loyal clients. Since the day she came across the ad offering an introductory session nearly twenty years ago, Mom has consulted the elderly woman on everything from which stocks to buy to when and where we should go on vacation. As if that's not enough, every year around my birthday, Mom drags me to see Auntie Xin for a fortune reading of my own.

Mom calls it a valuable gift.

I call it a waste of a perfectly good hour of my life.

Now that I am days from turning seventeen, we're seated across from Auntie Xin, separated by a wooden desk so large I'm convinced they knocked down a wall to move in. Despite this, we still barely meet the six-foot rule for social distancing. Of course, with Auntie Xin barely able to operate a smart phone, a virtual session was out of the question. Instead, we made the trip to see her in person, overheating from the double masks Mom insisted on using for the occasion.

"Are you sure?" Mom whispers.

The unnaturally black strands of Auntie Xin's bangs fall into her eyes as she squints at incomprehensible—to me, at least—lines of characters and numbers that combine to reveal my fortune. Auntie Xin leans back against her equally ancient chair, the wooden legs squeaking despite its featherlight occupant.

"I'm afraid so, Chan tàitài," she tells Mom. "I even read it against the Daymaster. I am certain. Your daughter will face great challenges this year."

Besides the global pandemic that has turned my junior year into a never-ending cycle of Zoom lectures and late-night essay writing? Or the highly depressing realization that my social life hasn't changed a bit since quarantine started?

I keep this all to myself . . . especially the last part. Even before COVID, Mom never failed to complain about how much time I spent at home. Of course, she was also the one who wouldn't let me leave without knowing who I was with, where I was going, and when I'd be back.

"What kind of challenges?" Mom asks, voice shaking. "Are you talking about the virus? Could she get sick?"

Auntie Xin consults her book once more, muttering under her breath as she flips between pages before heaving a long sigh.

"It's difficult to say exactly, but I've warned you about Michelle's weak immune system. That's why she's so small. She's prone to getting sick, so be extra careful."

I resist the urge to roll my eyes. It's bad enough that at five foot one, I'm the shortest one of my friends . . . maybe even the entire junior class of Memorial High. But it's genetics, not my chronic allergies, that forces me to shop for clothes in the kids' section. Besides Dad, no one on either side of my family can reach the top shelf at the grocery store.

"Should Michelle stop working at the restaurant, then?" Mom asks. "We had to let go of all our staff when this whole thing started, so she's been helping out."

Helping out is her way of saying I'm working for free six days a week . . . or as she puts it, for the privilege of having a roof over my head and clothes on my back. I hold my breath, hoping fortune will be on my side, but Auntie Xin shakes her head.

"As long as she is taking the herbs I recommended and following precautions, I don't see any reason she can't continue."

Great.

"Of course, Xin năinai. I always follow your advice to the letter," Mom assures. "I make sure she never misses a day."

This time, I can't keep the grimace off my face. I can still taste the nasty ocean seaweed powder I had to down in a glass of water this morning. No matter how much I stirred, it never dissolved like the container promised.

"Good, good. The herbs are proven to help boost health and vitality. In fact, you might want to pick some more up before you leave. I'm running low on supplies, and with everything on lockdown I don't know when I'll get more in."

I swallow a groan at how quickly Mom agrees to take all but one pack of the cursed regimen. Judging by the sparkle in her eyes, Auntie Xin is one *excellent* short of becoming a movie villain.

"There is some good news, though," she continues. "As long as Michelle stays focused, she will do very well in school."

I wince as Mom smacks me on the arm. "You hear that? Don't spend so much time on your phone. That's why your grades aren't good."

"Mom, I have straight As in all my classes," I whine. "How is that not good?"

"They are not high As. That's what you need to get the best scholarships," she immediately replies. "Unless you've changed your mind about going away for college."

I pretend not to hear the hopeful tone in her voice. Mom's been trying to convince me to pick a college close to home, but Pri has her heart set on UT Austin, and I'm not spending those four years without my best friend of ten years.

I shake my head. "No, I still want to go to UT."

"Michelle, there are plenty of great colleges near here. And Daddy and I can save money if you live at home . . ."

They could save money by not wasting it on those herbs she just bought, but I keep that to myself. Thankfully, Auntie Xin's egg timer goes off, preventing Mom from launching into a full-on campaign.

"Time's up for today," Auntie Xin says, closing her notebook. "Same time next week?"

Mom sighs. "Actually, I'm going to have to cancel next week's session. Business has finally picked up, but that means we're working more hours at the restaurant."

"I understand. It has been tough for us all these past few weeks. I will go ahead and cancel your session."

Auntie Xin flips to the appointments section of her notebook and scratches out Mom's name. As she goes to close it, she suddenly glances at me.

"Actually, since it's your birthday, I will let you ask one additional question before we finish today."

Mom opens her mouth, but Auntie Xin cuts her off by putting a hand up.

"I want Michelle to ask the question."

Both women turn to me, and I feel Mom's eyes boring holes in the side of my head. The seconds tick by, but nothing comes to mind.

"Um . . ."

"Hurry up, Michelle. Don't waste Xin nǎinai's time. She has other clients waiting," Mom chides.

Not helpful.

I rack my brain. What do people usually ask about? I've already heard about my health and school, and I'm sure as hell not expecting any money. Perhaps sensing my distress, or maybe in an attempt to get us out the door, Auntie Xin pipes up.

"What about love?"

I stare at her. "Love?"

"Wouldn't you like to know if you'll meet a nice boy this year?"

A very specific boy comes to mind almost immediately. One I've already met. Too bad he doesn't know I exist. Auntie Xin quirks one eyebrow at me, and I suddenly feel naked beneath her sharp gaze.

"Michelle doesn't have time to meet any boys," Mom interrupts, oblivious. "She's focusing on school."

Auntie Xin is too busy consulting her notes to hear her. Instead, she mutters to herself as she jots down some calculations. After a few minutes, she raises her head.

"Well, unfortunately, the path to love will be quite bumpy . . ."

Mom makes a satisfied sound beside me. Auntie Xin clears her throat.

"But if your companion is a rabbit, horse, or pig, you will reach your destination together."

"Oh no, that won't work. A rabbit would be too old, and a pig too young," Mom immediately jumps in to say.

"Horse it is, then," Auntie Xin replies, winking at me. "But be careful. One born in the winter is cold. He'll break your heart. Choose one born in spring or summer. Now, time to go."

Auntie Xin stands, ushering us back out to the front. Before we leave the shop, Mom reminds her of the bags of horrible herbs she promised to buy. Once she receives a plastic bag full of the instruments of my torture, she waves goodbye and we head to the car. After starting the engine, Mom turns to me.

"School first, Michelle. Boys later."

When I don't immediately answer, her eyes narrow.

"Okay, okay," I mumble. "School first."

"Good. Now, what do you want for dinner?"

———

"Thank you for calling Chan's Chinese Café. May I take your order?"

"I'm sorry, can you repeat that?" the person on the other end says. "I can't hear you."

I pull the phone closer to my mouth, cursing the way my mask muffles my words.

"Thank you for calling Chan's Chinese Café. What would you like to order?"

I scribble down the dishes as the customer rattles them off one by one.

"So that's one Kung Pao chicken, one pepper steak, and a combination fried rice. Your total is twenty-five dollars and six cents. It'll be ready in about fifteen to twenty minutes."

It's my birthday today, and so far I've spent it sitting through hours of Zoom lectures and then stuck at the restaurant. It's nearly time to close, but I'm surprised at how many orders are still coming in. I guess nothing makes you crave Chinese food like being stuck in your house twenty-four hours a day.

I've barely hung up when the phone rings again. This time, the customer doesn't know what they want, so I put them on speakerphone while they decide. I unlock my cell and open up Twitter, chuckling at the meme thread Pri just sent me. I'm so distracted that I don't hear the bell above the front door ding, or the footsteps as someone approaches the counter.

"Um, hi. I'm here to pick up a to-go order?"

I start, nearly dropping my phone. My eyes briefly meet a pair of deep brown ones peeking out from above a blue mask before I bow my head in apology.

"Yes, of course. What's the name for the order?"

"David."

I tap on the computer screen and scroll until I find his name.

"Okay, you had one order of egg rolls, hot and sour soup, sweet and sour shrimp, and sesame chicken with steamed rice, right?"

"Yup."

"Your total is thirty-two dollars and sixty-five cents."

He slides two twenty-dollar bills across the counter. I shake my head politely.

"I'm sorry, but we're only taking credit cards at this time."

"Oh, sure. Hold on a sec."

As he reaches for his wallet, I hear a discombobulated voice floating through the air.

"Hello? Hello!"

Oh no. The customer on the phone!

"I'm so sorry for the wait," I barely avoid shouting into the handset. "What would you like to order?"

Grabbing a pen, I take their order while gesturing toward the credit machine.

Credit or debit? I mouth to David.

"Credit."

I finish taking the phone order while he pays, sighing with relief after hanging up. When the machine spits out the store receipt, I tear it off and slide it toward him.

"Please sign this one for me."

As David signs on the dotted line, I take a good look at him for the first time. When my brain registers the absurdly long eyelashes, thick brows, and wavy black hair, my heart stops.

Oh my god.

It's him.

"You're not David," I blurt out.

His eyebrows shoot up. I groan inwardly before explaining.

"I recognize you. You're Evan . . . Evan Kwon."

Evan Kwon, the star of Memorial High's varsity swim team, nicknamed the Asian Michael Phelps because he tried out for the U.S. Olympic swim team (though he didn't make the cut). Even if he weren't six feet tall, his easygoing personality and ridiculously good looks would make him stand out in a crowd. He's also the boy I've been crushing on since I spotted him in the parking lot on the first day of freshman year.

"Um, yeah. That's me."

When several seconds pass without Evan saying anything else, I realize something.

He has no idea who I am.

"We . . . we go to the same school," I finally say, eyes pinned on his right earlobe. "We had chemistry together."

Something I'm reminded we don't actually have as he stares at me blankly.

"I mean, chemistry class. We had chemistry class. Together."

"Oh. I didn't realize . . ."

This is just getting worse by the minute. Wishing I could summon the earth to swallow me whole, I print out a copy of his receipt and hold it out. He accepts it without a word, and I grab his order and place it on the counter. As he reaches for it, he tips his head to the side, his mahogany eyes narrowing slightly.

"Wait . . . I think I do know you."

I endure another moment of scrutiny before his eyes light up. My traitorous mind fills in the teasing grin hidden behind his mask, and suddenly it's hard to breathe.

"Michelle, right?"

I nod, not trusting my voice.

"You're the one who made those fireballs for your final project, right? With the seeds?"

"Spores," I correct. "Lycopodium spores. They're super flammable when you mix them with air."

"Oh, yeah. Well, it was super cool."

It would've been nicer if he said *I* was cool, but at least he remembers my name. He inhales as if to say something else, but pauses when his cellphone goes off. He checks the screen before heaving a sigh.

"That's my dad. I should go."

"Okay, sure. Have a good night," I stammer. "Enjoy your dinner."

"I'm sure we will. It smells amazing."

Evan picks up his food and walks toward the door. As he goes to push it open, he glances back at me.

"I'll see you around."

I'm still staring at the door minutes later when Mom sticks her head out of the kitchen and shoots me an irritated look.

"Michelle! What are you doing out there?"

"Huh?"

"The phone, Michelle. Why aren't you picking it up? It's been ringing nonstop."

"Oh, sorry!"

She watches me like a hawk as I answer the call.

"Thank you for calling Chan's Chinese Café. What would you like to order?"

———

The following Saturday, I'm counting down the minutes until we close after a hellish day of wrong orders, customers refusing to wear masks, and even a small kitchen fire. That's not counting the number of times food delivery app drivers mistook me for a middle schooler and asked to speak to my parents. The only thing that kept me from quitting was watching the hilarious TikToks Pri kept sending me. She keeps trying to convince me to do one with her, but just the thought of someone at school seeing it gives me hives.

Even the sight of Evan walking through the door half an hour before nine does little to brighten my mood. Dressed simply in a sky blue T-shirt emblazoned with our school mascot and a pair of shorts, the lower half of his face covered by another blue mask, he still manages to look like he stepped off a magazine shoot. He follows the makeshift path we created by stacking chairs atop tables and comes to a stop in front of me. I tilt my head up to meet his gaze.

"Hi," I say, smiling shyly. "Picking up another order?"

He grins. Or at least, his eyes do, forming twin crescents as he nods.

"And it's under Evan this time."

I quickly pull up the information on the computer, grateful my hand is steady despite the mad drumming of my heart.

"Just egg drop soup and broccoli beef with brown rice?"

"Yup. My parents are at the hospital, so it's just me tonight."

I turn to him, eyes wide. "Oh my god! Are they okay? How are you doing?"

He doesn't respond for a full second. Then he bursts out laughing, waving his hands in front of him.

"No, no, I'm sorry! I should've explained better. My parents *work* at the hospital. They're both doctors at St. Mark's."

"Oh! That's good!" I swallow a groan. "I mean, it's not good that they're working at the hospital. Good that they're not sick."

"I know what you meant," he assures me. "And I'm glad they're not sick too. But they started working a lot more this week, so I haven't seen them in a few days."

The light dims slightly in his eyes, and I suddenly feel very lucky to have Mom and Dad in the next room.

"You must miss them."

He shrugs. "I mean, I'm kind of used to it since they've always been busy. But this is different, you know?"

There's a mixture of worry and sadness in his voice. I resist the urge to reach across the counter, and ball my fists at my sides instead.

"What kind of doctors are they?"

"My dad is an ER doctor, and my mom's a pediatrician."

"Have they seen a lot of COVID cases?"

"Yeah, and it's really bad. They say the public has no idea how serious things are. Mom came home crying yesterday after one of the kids she took care of didn't make it."

My heart clenches. "Oh, wow. That sounds so tough."

Silence falls between us. Unsure of what to say next, I gesture toward the kitchen.

"I'll go check and see if your food's ready."

"I'll be here."

I push my way through the swinging metal door and step into the kitchen. Dad's standing at the stove, one hand gripped tightly around the handle of the wok he's working while ladling a small amount of chicken stock over the meat and vegetables cooking within. Nearby, Mom's busy transferring the orders that are ready into the black plastic to-go containers she's placed in a line to speed things up. I pick my way past the center island to peek over her shoulder.

"What are you looking for, Michelle?" Mom asks without turning.

"Um, broccoli beef with brown rice."

She tosses her head toward Dad. "I think that's what he's got in the wok right now."

"Do you want me to get the soup ready for the order?" I volunteer.

I take her grunt as an affirmative and move to the large black pots we keep the soups warm in. I carefully scoop in a portion of the egg drop soup and seal the plastic lid, bringing it to the window that separates the kitchen from the dining room. Evan waves at me from the other side, and a giggle escapes my lips.

"What are you laughing about?"

I turn to Mom. "Nothing. I just . . . thought of a joke."

She frowns, but I rush out of the kitchen before she has a chance to ask any questions. I circle around and grab the egg drop soup off the sill, placing it on the counter before adding napkins and a condiment. As I reach for the utensils, I pause.

"Um . . . do you want me to include a fork and knife too?"

His brows furrow, and somehow, I know he's pouting under that mask. Of course, it could also be the countless number of hours I spent pretending I wasn't studying every inch of his face during class.

"I know I was a disaster during chem lab, Michelle, but I promise I know how to use chopsticks responsibly."

He sounds so offended that I immediately regret my words.

"Oh, I didn't mean to imply . . ."

I freeze as he burst into laughter. "I'm just playing with you. Chopsticks are fine."

At a loss for words, I finish adding the rest of the items to his bag just as the bell we use to signal the food is ready goes off behind me. I turn and find Mom eyeing Evan, her expression a cross between curiosity and suspicion. As I reach up to grab the broccoli beef off the counter, she puts a hand over mine.

"Who's that?"

I force myself to hold her gaze. "Just a classmate from school."

"Why is he here?"

I point at the container between us with my chin.

"He's picking up a to-go order. That's his food."

She immediately relaxes. "Oh. Well, make sure you pack it well."

Mom leans to the side and smiles politely at him. "Thank you for ordering. We appreciate your business."

"You're welcome, ma'am," he answers. "My parents love the food here. We grab dinner from here at least once a week. They say it's the best in the city."

The smile on Mom's face relaxes into a genuine one. "Thank you so much! We take great pride in using only the freshest ingredients."

"It definitely shows. Everything I've tried here has been delicious."

"Well, you'll have to thank them for me. Better yet, you should all dine in once this is over. I'd love to meet them."

"I will definitely tell them to do that, ma'am."

Mom makes a disgruntled sound. "What's this ma'am business? Call me Mrs. Chan."

"Of course, Mrs. Chan."

She turns to me. "Why haven't you packed that up? I don't want his food to get cold."

She disappears into the kitchen as I tuck the sealed container beneath his soup. When I glance up, she hands me a small white foam box.

"Tell him these egg rolls are on the house."

I press my lips together to keep from laughing. Only Evan can charm someone as wary as Mom in less than a minute.

"I will."

As I turn to walk the food over to him, I hear Mom muttering in the background.

"Such a nice boy . . . so polite . . ."

As I hand Evan his food, he tips his head toward the kitchen.

"Is that your mom?"

"Yeah."

"She seems nice."

I cock my eyebrow, and he chuckles.

"She can't be that bad."

"Let's just say I don't get free egg rolls from her, and we're related."

"No way! I got them for free?" He looks past me into the kitchen. "Thank you for the egg rolls, Mrs. Chan!"

Her head pops up so fast I'm convinced she was hiding just out of sight.

"You're welcome! Don't forget to tell your parents to come by next time!"

"I totally will!" he calls out.

Right then, Evan's stomach grumbles so loudly we both hear it. Rather than being embarrassed, he just laughs.

"Guess that means I should get going."

"Yeah. You should eat that while it's still hot," I agree. "Especially the egg rolls. They don't taste good soggy."

He nods, but doesn't turn to leave. In fact, he lingers, watching me expectantly . . . almost as if he wants . . .

"Um . . . don't you need me to pay for the food?"

"Right! Of course!"

Of course he was waiting to pay, Michelle. What did you think he wanted?

I mumble a farewell after handing him the paper and watch him head toward the door. Shortly after he leaves, we close up the restaurant and jump in the car to head home. In the darkness, Mom twists in her seat and proceeds to pepper me with questions about Evan. When I tell her about his parents, she lets out a sympathetic sound.

"That poor boy! No wonder he's so skinny! Next time he comes, make sure you tell me so I can send him home with a little extra food."

"Okay, Mom. I will."

"He seems like maybe he needs someone to talk to too. You should get to know him better. Maybe you two can be friends."

I choke back a laugh. Of the many things Evan does not lack, it's friends. He's usually surrounded by them.

Then again, if she is encouraging me to talk to him, who am I to complain?

—

There must be something special about Mom's egg rolls, because true to his word, Evan starts stopping by the restaurant nearly every night. Each time, he comes by around half an hour before closing.

On the third day, Mom suggests that he wait to order his food until he's here so that it's as fresh as possible.

"You're welcome to pull up a chair and wait," she tells him. "We only keep them put up so people know there's no dine-in."

"Are you sure that's okay? I don't want to get in the way," he answers.

"Nonsense! As you can see, it's just the three of us here. Most people don't order food this late at night anyway. Michelle will keep you company while you wait."

I'll do what now?

Mom shoots me a meaningful look as she passes by me on the way to the kitchen. Well, it *would* be meaningful, anyway, if I knew what she was trying to tell me.

"Be nice," she whispers.

Yeah, that still tells me nothing.

Once Evan and I are alone, I clear my throat. "Uh . . . how are your parents?"

Good start. Solid start.

"I think they're okay," he answers, dragging a hand through his thick hair. "They've actually started staying in a hotel near the hospital because they're worried about exposing me to the virus."

"Oh."

Okay, maybe not such a good topic of conversation.

"How's the training for swim team going?"

He looks at me like I've grown two heads. "We aren't training. You know, because of the whole social distancing thing?"

Strike two.

I sigh. "I'm sorry. I'm not very good at this."

"At what?"

"Talking to people."

Especially when said person happens to be as perfect as you.

"It's not really that hard," he says with a chuckle. "You just take turns asking questions and answering them."

"That's easy for you to say. It comes naturally to you."

I don't mean for it to sound as harsh as it does, but Evan

remains unbothered. Instead, he leans back in the chair and folds his arms over his chest.

"You just have to practice. Here, ask me a question."

"I just did," I deadpan. "Two, in fact."

He rolls his eyes. "An easier question. Something you would like to know about me."

Besides how you manage to look hot and cute at the exact same time?

"Have you always wanted to swim competitively?" I ask out loud instead.

Evan ponders this for a moment, the squint of his eyes reminding me of the way he would also pucker his lips while concentrating in chem lab.

Focus, Michelle.

"No. I actually started by accident. My parents wanted to keep me busy during the summer, so they put me in swim classes at the local pool." He shifts in his seat. "My teacher at the time was a former competitive swimmer, and I guess he saw something in me. He talked them into enrolling me in private lessons with him. The rest is history."

"Were your parents disappointed when you didn't pass the Olympic trials?"

He shrugs slightly. "Maybe a little, but I'm lucky that they've always supported me no matter what. And to be honest, I'm kind of glad I didn't make the cut. Training at that level takes up so much time. It doesn't leave room for anything else."

"Do you know what you want to do after you graduate, then?" I ask.

"I'm not sure yet. I was hoping to figure that out this year, but then COVID happened."

The mention of the virus spreading rampantly through Houston turns our mood somber. We sit in silence, wrapped in our own thoughts. After a while, Evan leans forward and smiles.

"Now it's your turn. What do you want to do after graduation?"

"Oh, um, I'm hoping I'll get into UT Austin. They have a really good pre-med program."

"That's pretty awesome," he comments, sounding impressed. "Not everyone can go into medicine."

"Yeah, well, we'll see if I can cut it."

"I mean, you set the curve in chemistry while I nearly blew up the lab, so how much harder could med school be?"

I hum. "I suppose you have a point."

Our eyes meet across the designated six feet of space, and we burst into laughter at the same time. We're still chuckling when Mom appears, carrying his order in one hand. Evan pops out of his chair as Mom places it on the nearest table.

"There you go. Egg drop soup, walnut shrimp, and of course, egg rolls. I also threw in some of our special lo mein."

"That's too much, Mrs. Chan," he protests. "I can't accept this."

Mom pushes it toward him. "I insist. If you don't take it, I'll be very upset."

Evan quickly acquiesces. "Well, I wouldn't want that. Thank you, really."

She walks him to the door, unlocking it to let him out.

"We'll see you tomorrow?"

His eyes flicker over to me, and he winks.

"I'll be here."

—

Three weeks pass by in the blink of an eye, and by the end of it, I've learned more random facts about Evan than I ever expected to.

His favorite color is green. Not bright green, but deep green, like moss.

He's allergic to cats, but still owns two.

He was born left-handed, but his parents trained him to use his right instead.

Even though he's really good at swimming, the only other sport he can play is soccer.

He gets his height from his paternal grandfather, who passed away before he was born.

As we keep talking, Evan starts revealing other things, things that make me realize there's so much more to him than what he shows others.

He wishes he were smarter, like his older brother, who is attending law school.

Even though he has a lot of friends, he doesn't feel close to any of them.

He really enjoys learning, and will sometimes spend an entire day wandering through a museum.

Lately, he's been up late at night worrying about his parents.

The more time we spend together, the harder it is to ignore the way my heart dances when Evan teases me about something I said, or the warmth that spreads through me whenever he laughs so hard his shoulders shake. Soon, he's the first thing that pops up in my head when I wake, and the last thing I think about before I shut my eyes.

The worst part of it all, though, is the fact that I'm still not positive he feels the same way. Pri's convinced he does, but I'm reluctant to get my hopes up. Sure, I've lost count of the number of winks he's given me, and I've caught him staring at me on occasion. Beyond that, though, there's always a distance between us he never quite closes.

Maybe Mom's right. Maybe Evan just wants someone to talk to.

"Michelle? Michelle."

I start as something touches my shoulder, and glance over to find Evan's hand. I follow his arm up until I reach his deep brown eyes. For a breath, I see something flit across his features, but I blink and it's gone. He grabs a chair and pushes it toward me.

"Sorry," I mumble, sliding it under the table. "What were you saying?"

Today was the first day the city opened back up, and I've spent the day setting up the dining room for a limited number of dine-in customers. When Evan arrived to order as usual, Mom invited him to stay and have dinner with us instead.

"I was asking if you had any plans this summer," he repeats.

"No. Even if COVID wasn't happening, my parents don't really take any time off. The restaurant business is year-round."

"They don't even close for the holidays?"

I shake my head. "Nope. That's usually when we're the busiest."

"Oh. I guess that makes sense."

"In fact, the day you came in to pick up your dad's to-go order was my birthday."

Evan's eyes widen. "You were working on your birthday?"

"Yeah, but they did get me a cake," I feel compelled to add.

He glances toward the kitchen as the sound of sizzling oil and clanging pots reaches our ears. Since it's just the four of us, we're maskless, for once, something I discover is both a blessing and a curse every time he flashes one of his signature teasing smiles.

At the moment, however, he's watching me with a strange expression on his face.

"Well, since I'm part of the reason you were stuck at work on your birthday," he says slowly, "why don't I make it up to you?"

"Technically, I was already scheduled to work that day, so you don't really owe me anything," I assure him.

"Oh."

Evan's face falls as he slumps against the back of his chair. I realize belatedly that was not the reaction he was expecting. My heart starts to pound, but I work to keep my voice even.

"Why? What did you have in mind?"

Evan's eyes snap up to meet mine. He sits up straight and swallows.

"Well, there's a special exhibit about ancient Egypt coming to the Museum of Natural Science. They brought some of the artifacts found in King Tut's tomb. They're only letting in a few people at a time each day, so I thought maybe . . . we could check it out together. That is, if you want. We can also do something else."

"No, no! It sounds really interesting." I take a deep breath. "I'd love to go."

He brightens immediately. "Great! I'll figure out when the exhibit starts."

Evan grins, and I can't help but return it. Suddenly feeling shy, I clear my throat.

"What about you? Did you do anything to celebrate your birthday?"

He nods. "We normally take a family vacation during winter break."

Something about that nags at me, but I can't figure out why. I hear a gasp and turn to find Mom frozen to the spot, a plate of fried eggplant sitting precariously in her hands.

"Did you say . . . winter?"

Evan frowns. "Um, yes?"

"Sounds lovely," Mom replies, though her voice is an octave higher than normal. "Michelle, we need your help in the kitchen."

"Now?"

"Yes, now," she says, smiling tightly.

"Okay . . ."

I stand and follow her back to the kitchen. Once we're hidden from view, Mom turns and hisses at me.

"I don't want you spending any more time with Evan."

I stare at her. "What? Why?"

Dad pokes his head out from behind the refrigerator door. "What's going on?"

"Nothing. Go back to cooking," Mom commands before turning her attention back to me. "Don't you remember who Auntie Xin warned you about?"

Everything suddenly clicks into place, and I groan loudly.

"Mom, just because she mentioned a winter horse doesn't mean she was talking about Evan."

"No, it has to be him," she insists stubbornly. "There's no one else that fits her reading, and I won't give him the chance to break your heart."

"Mom, wait!"

Before I can stop her, she stomps back out into the dining room. I rush behind her as she walks up to a startled Evan.

"I'm sorry, Evan. I'm afraid something's come up," Mom lies. "We'll have to postpone dinner to another night."

Evan looks at me questioningly, but I avert my gaze. I know better than to contradict her right now. Though he says nothing at first, Evan eventually nods and stands.

"Of course, I totally understand." He peers at me. "I'll text you later?"

"Actually, Michelle's going to be pretty busy with finals

soon," Mom interjects. "I'd appreciate it if you don't bother her while she's studying."

His mouth falls open. "I don't under—"

"Don't worry. I'll pack the food up for you," she continues, undeterred. "I wouldn't want you to go home hungry."

With that, she clamps a hand onto my wrist and drags me with her. I manage to throw a single, desperate glance back before we disappear through the swinging metal doors. With one eye pinned on me, Mom packs the food into to-go containers before taking it up to the front. I turn to Dad, but he shrugs helplessly.

"You know how your mom gets about those readings. There's no stopping her."

Out of options, all I can do is watch as Mom shuffles Evan out the door and out of my life.

—

To make sure I don't defy her wishes, Mom takes my phone away the minute I get home. Thankfully, she leaves my laptop for school, but she forces me to use it out in the living room. She even hires one of the old staff to work at the restaurant so she can stay home with me. Despite this, I'm able to secretly message Evan through Twitter and apologize for Mom's behavior.

Was it something I said? Or did?

No, I type back. *You didn't do anything wrong. Things are just a little . . . complicated right now.*

For several minutes, all that appears at the bottom of the chat are three little dots. Then, a single question appears.

Do you still want to go to the museum with me?

Hours later, I still don't have a good answer for him. Tucked into my favorite armchair, I'm pretending to work on the essay part of my English final. In reality, I'm asking Pri for advice about what to do. I know leaving Evan on read for so long wasn't fair, but this isn't an easy decision to make. If I sneak out of the house and Mom finds out, I'll be grounded for life.

A notification appears on my screen. It's a message from Pri.

Pick a day and I'll cover for you. Tell your mom we're meeting up at the museum to work on our art final.

I minimize the tab as soon as Mom walks past. The minute she walks down the hall, however, I open up Twitter again. Keeping one eye on the doorway, I type a quick reply.

I owe you, girl.

Yup, she sends back. *You owe me big.*

Firstborn child?

You know it.

I chuckle. *Done.*

The next message I send is to Evan.

Is it too late to say yes?

I hold my breath as I stare at the screen. Fifteen long minutes later, I have his answer. It makes me smile.

Depends. Is tomorrow too soon?

One hurdle down. One very big one to go.

After practicing my speech several times in my head, I find Mom in the laundry room.

"Mom? Can I meet up with Pri tomorrow so we can work on our art final?"

She eyes me with immediate suspicion. "Why can't she just come here?"

"We're supposed to pick a famous painting and write an essay analyzing it," I answer. "The one we picked out is on display at the Museum of Fine Art."

"Why today? Why can't you go later this week?"

"The project is due by Friday, and tomorrow is the only day Pri can go. Plus, the museum has free admission as long as we reserve a spot."

I've said the magic word. *Free.*

"Okay, but you need to be home by dinner," Mom says. "I don't want you going anywhere else either. Understood?"

"Perfectly."

The next afternoon, I don my mask and take the car to the Museum of Fine Art. I pull into the parking garage and head up to the lobby, where Pri is waiting. We snap a quick picture to send to Mom, and then she hugs me tight.

"Have fun."

While she heads home, I cut through Hermann Park to reach the Museum of Natural Science. Usually, the museum district is packed full of visitors enjoying the nice weather and free admission. Today, there's only the occasional family moving along the sidewalks. When I reach my destination, I spy Evan right away, standing literally head and shoulders above the other museumgoers in line to get inside. As I approach, he greets me with a wave. Like me, he's wearing a mask, but my stomach does a little flip anyway.

"Hey."

"Hi," I answer back.

"You ready?"

I nod, and we make our way into the open-air lobby. The normally bare concrete floor is now marked with bright neon tape, indicating where visitors can stand while maintaining social distance. Evan shows the attendant the tickets he purchased before coming, and we're handed an information booklet and put into a queue for entry.

Once it's our turn, we're ushered into a dimly lit room, where another attendant directs us to the first numbered display. After we check out a few displays, Evan taps me on the shoulder, gesturing toward a small alcove. We find two seats on a bench in the back and sit down as a short film plays on a projector. When the only other person inside walks out, Evan scoots closer.

"I'm glad you came." His words are slow, hesitant. "Considering what happened the other day, I didn't know if you . . ."

"Would want to meet up?"

He nods. Impulsively, perhaps spurred by the courage one only finds in darkness, I reach out and touch his forearm. He tenses, and I instantly regret it. I pull away and clasp my hands in my lap.

"I owe you an explanation for what happened the other day. It's just kind of hard to put into words."

"I'm a good listener," he says with a gentle smile.

I heave a sigh. "Okay. My mom is very superstitious. Like, go-see-a-fortune-teller-every-week kind of superstitious. Every year, she makes me go with her to get a birthday fortune. This time, the fortune-teller said I might find . . . um, love."

I pause, cheeks flaming. "But she also warned me that a winter horse would break my heart."

Evan looks confused. "Your mom sent me away because I mentioned winter?"

"Yes." I reach up with my free hand to fiddle with my earring. "Not that it justifies how she acted, but Mom thought she was protecting me."

"Do *you* believe what the fortune-teller said?" he asks after a beat.

"I—" I take a deep breath. "No, I'm not like my mom. I'm not superstitious, but . . ."

"But?"

"No one wants to get their heart broken," I admit.

"I don't think anyone does," he agrees softly.

I drum up the courage to look up at him. There's a lot to decipher in those dark brown eyes, but the uncertainty I find in them mirrors my own. Evan looks away, brows furrowed as he swallows hard. His hand inches across the bench, pausing halfway in the space between us.

It's an invitation, and just like when we were messaging, he's waiting patiently for me to accept.

I place my hand in his and thread our fingers together. He smiles, and I do too. We stay like this for as long as we dare, savoring the moment before leaving behind the privacy of the alcove to explore the rest of the exhibit.

Standing before a replica display of King Tut's tomb paintings, Evan suddenly turns to me with a frown.

"I still can't believe your mom got upset over my family's winter vacation."

I shake my head. "It's not that. It's because you have a winter birthday."

"Wait . . . *that's* what you meant by a winter horse?"

I nod, and I'm stunned when he throws his head back and laughs. The museum attendant glares in our direction, and I poke Evan in the side.

"What's so funny?"

"I wasn't born in the winter," he explains. "My birthday's in July. The reason we celebrate during winter break is because that's when my parents can take time off from work."

"*What?*" I stare at him, incredulous. "You've got to be kidding me! I just risked being grounded for life to come here!"

"Oh, come on, it can't really be that bad," he counters. "I'm sure your mom will forgive you."

"Says the guy she kicked out of our restaurant over a birthday."

He bursts into laughter again. This time, the other visitors join in frowning at us. I give Evan a warning look, but all he does is lean closer.

"Does that mean you have to get home soon?"

I can hear the pout in his voice. I find myself smiling.

"If I'm getting grounded anyway, I might as well enjoy my last moments of freedom."

Evan grins, the crinkle of his eyes enough to send my heart skittering. His hand tightens around mine.

"Then what are we waiting for?"

The Green Thumb War

by Brittney Morris

BILLIE VS. THE PLANTS

Normally, my therapist is pretty chill. Even when I tell her how cluttered and sad my brain is.

But not today.

Today, she recommended that I take up a new hobby, like juggling or hula hooping, or moving my favorite reading spot from my bedroom to the bay window in the living room. *Anything* to get me some fresh air and some of this "lovely spring sunshine we've been having," she says.

So, here I am, pausing in the fourth-floor stairwell to catch my breath, lugging a crate full of tiny green herb starter plants that will be dead by the end of the week. Somehow, I've managed to nourish myself for sixteen years, and keep my cat Ruby alive for nine, but everything else that comes home with me dies. Especially plants.

They say plants can sense good people and thrive when they're around them. Maybe deep down, I'm just not a good person. Maybe I just don't deserve them.

No, Billie, I tell myself, hoisting the crate up into my arms and starting up the stairs again, *stop that deprecating self-talk. What would Jordyn say?*

Jordyn, my therapist, would probably say that it's okay to catch myself talking down to myself, and that I can't course-correct until I notice I'm off-course.

So here I go, up the stairs, quietly course-correcting.

I reach our apartment door, set the little plants down, and unlock it. Ruby meows at me from her favorite spot in the window, and as I heave the carton of plants through the door and set them down on the kitchen table, I smile.

"Hey, fluffy girl," I say, shrugging out of my hoodie and tucking my hair behind my ear. I scoop her fat ass up in my arms and nuzzle my face in her white and orange fur. She squirms out of my arms and slinks her way back up onto the window.

"Glad you see you too, Rubles," I say. I look past her and out the window. There's a sad little planter box just on the other side, covered in spiderwebs, dead roots, and what I'm pretty sure is the remains of a bird's nest.

From like three years ago.

And I sigh, because all I want to do is kick off my shoes

and socks, slip into some shorts, curl up in bed with a cup of tea and a good book and Ruby on my lap, and read my troubles away.

But I can't.

Because I'm now the mother of a tarragon plant, a cilantro plant, a basil plant, and a parsley plant, and they can't survive on the kitchen table all afternoon.

So I roll up my sleeves and get to it, wondering why I forced myself into this. I slip on some rubber kitchen gloves—because we don't have gardening ones, because nobody's gardened here since before we moved in—and I start scooping. All of the old gray soil that's been caking itself into bricks in the planter basket for years goes straight into the paper bag in my hand, handful by dusty handful.

I think of how much cheaper a hula hoop would've been. And then I remember I can't hula hoop.

I think of how much easier it would've been to find things around the house to juggle. And then I remember we live on the fifth floor and the neighbors below us get mad if we walk around too angrily in socks.

So I sigh, and I keep scooping.

Putting in the new soil is actually kind of . . . I won't say fun . . . *interesting*. It feels soft and lush under my gloved fingers. So soft that I actually decide to take the gloves off and feel the dirt.

It's strangely . . . nice.

And then . . .

THE WILD BARKING OF AN UNTAMED CANINE!

I nearly drop the bag of soil the whole five stories to the ground below and brace myself against the sill to keep from falling out the window. Ruby is freaking the hell out, fur sky-high off her back and tail and claws dug into the bay window cushion.

My fear gives way to rage as I look out the window and across the eight-foot gap between where I stand and the next building over, at the wild fluffy mutt in the window barking away at my sweet Ruby darling. The dog owned by none other than the menace next door sitting at his desk: Sebastian.

I only know his name from all the times I've called the front desk about this yapping dog—more times than I can remember—and yet here he still is, harassing my poor kitty baby.

I growl and consider slamming the window shut. That's what I'd normally do. But I look down at my little plant babies—I'm already kind of getting attached to them, I'll admit it—and decide that if I'm going to get through planting all four of them, I have to end that racket.

Now.

"Hey!" I holler out the window. But Sebastian is wearing enormous headphones over his black curls, shirtless with his back turned to me at his desk. *Ruby* doesn't like me yelling, though, apparently, because she panics. Her claws dig into the windowsill, her fur stands on end, her tail coils up against her ass like a corkscrew, and she yeets herself across the gap between my apartment and the building next door.

"*Ruby!*" I holler, reaching out for her.

But it's too late.

She lands on Sebastian's windowsill and leaps inside onto the carpet. The dog lunges at her, and she jumps off his closet door and runs straight into the desk lamp, shattering it into pieces.

Oh shit.

But Sebastian doesn't flinch.

Seriously?

I stare, mouth agape at how oblivious this boy is while his dog and my cat chase each other around his room.

"Ruby, come back, girl, it's okay!" I holler again, irritated at how ironic it is that now *I've* become the loud one. His headphones must be noise-canceling because he doesn't turn around. At all. Instead he bends down and fluffs his dog's fur, then looks at the floor, follows the trail of glass over to his desk, and then up to the broken desk lamp.

Before I can react or think to warn him, he's getting up— no wait, he's barefoot! He stumbles backward, holding his foot, and goes careening into his closet with a crash.

He groans with pain. I cover my mouth with my hands and freeze where I am, looking guilty as hell, just as he looks up and out the window at me. I can't move. I want to run away and disappear forever to save myself from this embarrassment. But I also need my cat back.

As if she can hear my thoughts, she bounds back into view in the window, up onto Sebastian's sill, and across the gap.

I catch her in my arms and in one fell swoop, I set Ruby on the bay window seat, slam the window shut, run to my room, and dive under the covers.

I hope I never have to see that boy again.

And I hope he's okay.

SEBASTIAN VS. THE PITS

It's been three weeks since I've been able to sit at my keyboard and play.

I didn't really care that I needed stitches in my foot after they took out the glass, or that I shattered my wrist and needed surgery after I went flying into my own closet.

Or I *wouldn't* have cared if my arm cast had stopped at my elbow.

But no, Mr. Doctor Man just *had* to go halfway up my humerus, leaving my arm stuck at an awkward L-shape for the rest of the summer, *right* before I was about to learn to play "Killing in the Name."

I light the candle sitting on the sheet music stand and watch the flame flicker while the scent of citronella fills my room. That scent always chills me out. Reminds me of sitting around in the communal garden and staving off the early summer mosquitoes. My mom got me into aromatherapy for a science project I did in the fifth grade, and it just kinda . . . stuck.

I sigh and look just past the candle, at Hopscotch in his terrarium.

"You don't care, huh?" I smile at the frog. "Long as I have one good hand so I can play with you."

I reach in and pick him up gently, feeling his slippery little body settle into the palm of my right hand as he blinks one eye, then the other, in hello.

He doesn't ribbit much anymore since he's old now, but I can look at his eyes and know when he's smiling at me.

And right now, he's smiling.

"Yeah, man, you're right," I say, setting him back inside next to his water pot. "Gotta keep positive."

As if on cue, the fluffy little mop of chaos in the family bolts through the door and jumps up on my leg, panting up at me.

"Yo, Oscar, I'm a little laid-up now, you cain't just be runnin' up on me like that." But I laugh and floof his snow white fur. I can't stay mad at him.

And then I look up at the windowsill, at my third species of little ones to take care of. My plants. Specifically, my herbs—sage, rosemary, lavender, and oregano. I've never taken care of plants before. But they're quieter than dogs, they're cleaner than frogs, and they only need three things: water, sunlight, and company.

I scoot my keyboard seat up to the planter box outside the window and look down at them all. Arthur—my therapist, and feelings organizer extraordinaire—told me that talking to them can help fill in the gaps he can't fill virtually, especially now that I've gone and injured myself and can't go out for walks as often as I'd like. It just hasn't been the same meeting with him over video call. I can't sit on that huge emerald couch in his living room with the peach walls and the fresh plants, the soft sound of running water in the fountain on the coffee table, or the faint scent of eucalyptus—he's into aromatherapy, too.

But here, in my almost-empty room, where all my anxieties sit with me 24/7, where I lie awake at night catastrophizing everything while Mom is out driving for people all day? How am I supposed to relax here?

So I fold my arms on the sill and look at my little green friends. Mr. Lavender is coming in nicely, but he grows slow so he won't be ready until the end of summer, while Mrs. Oregano is already sprouted and ready to go. I lean down and smell her—that herby, delicious smell that I'm used to sprinkling in dried form over pizza.

"But that's a disgraceful fate for a plant as pretty as you, huh, ma'am? You deserve to be used for something greater, fresher. Not sure what that is yet, but—"

The sound of a sliding window catches me off guard, and I look up to see—for the first time in three weeks—the girl across the gap. That's what Mom calls the space between our buildings—the gap. The girl looks about my age, with the bell-shaped curls that brush her shoulders when she turns each page of whatever book she's reading. The one with the round face and the eyes as big and dark as wine grapes and sparkly as marbles.

"Hey," she says, leaning on the windowsill and clasping her hands together as if she has more to say. She's looking down at me with a piercing stare, and I can't tell if she's mad or nervous or something else.

"Hey," I say back, leaning on my windowsill, too, and nodding at her planter box. "Nice plants. What kind?"

She seems to prickle at my question, but then she glances down at them.

"Just . . . some starters I picked up at the nursery," she says with a sigh, cradling her hands around her elbows. "I came out here to say uh . . . sorry." She pauses for a minute, and I must stare in confusion for long enough that she realizes I have no idea what she's talking about, because she shrugs and continues. "For . . . your arm."

"Oh."

I don't hold it against her. I know cats aren't easy to control. It's why dogs are better. All they want to do is eat and play. I can relate. Unless . . . this girl *sicced* her cat on me? Or, for all I know, she might've been trying to flirt with me. I'm historically bad at realizing when someone's flirting vs. messing with me.

"It's fine now," I lie with a smile. "Had time to recover. Enough to take up planting these guys. I was just out here talking to them, by the way. You ever talk to yours?"

"Nah." She smirks. "Mine are too young. Don't think their ears have grown in yet."

No idea what she's talking about. They look like they're bursting right out of the planter box like a miniature jungle.

"They look almost ready for harvest to me," I say, craning my neck to get a better look at them. "What is that, basil?"

"That was a joke," she says, a bit coldly. "Why are you so interested in my plants anyway? Thought you had your own to worry about."

"Well, I think that joke was pretty *corny*," I say, with the hollowest silence between us in reply. "You know, because . . . I thought you meant you were growing . . . ears of . . . corn . . . Never mind."

"Anyway, I just came out here to apologize," she says, turning to pull the window closed. "This doesn't mean we're friends."

"Doesn't it?" I ask, before she can leave, "Or . . . wait . . . ohhhh, I get it."

This seems to pique her interest.

"What?" she asks with a frown.

"You must be intimidated by my awesome gardening skills," I say. Playing with her is strangely entertaining. It's like poking a bear that's stuck in a building at least ten feet away, a bear that I'll probably never see again after today if I keep poking her like this. All the entertainment with zero risk.

"I don't get *intimidated*," she says, a hint of a smile playing at the corner of her mouth for the first time today. "Certainly not by someone with such awful taste in pets."

Ouch.

I mean, not really. Oscar is awesome. I don't need nobody to tell me that. But that's a personal attack right there. That's my *son* she just dissed. I can't sleep tonight if I don't strike back—what, and miss an opportunity for free entertainment? Not I.

"Well, what if I don't get intimidated by cat people who sit around reading all day?" I ask.

Her face goes flat with horror.

"So you've been spying on me," she states. "I've never heard someone insult someone by admitting that."

"Like some kind of creep? Nah, I just happened to notice, you know? It's like living in a house by the beach and not expecting me to marvel at the view on a clear day."

I realize too late what I'm saying, and I feel my face go hot with embarrassment.

Oscar runs over and nibbles at my foot as if to say the same thing I'm thinking: *Great going, genius. This is why you don't have any friends.* But I take a deep breath and remember what Arthur said about fighting the pits. *Oftentimes it takes a fight.*

"I've got to go," she says.

"Wait," I say. There's *no* way I can leave this conversation having just admitted to her that I think she's ... well ... a view worth marveling at on a clear day. God, I cringe at how that sounds. Like bootleg Shakespeare. "Just going to leave without telling me your name?"

"Names are for people you plan to see again," she says. This girl is pure *ice* inside. But it intrigues me, so I keep on. I've got nothing to lose. She already thinks I have horrible taste in pets and zero poetic talent. Besides, I've got all afternoon.

"Or for people you *hope* to see again," I say.

Nice, I think. This time, *her* cheeks go pink, and I smile triumphantly. She frowns, rolls her eyes. "Billie," she says. "Yes, I'm sure it can be a girl's name. In fact, it's the name of the girl you could learn from in the gardening department. You know, because she reads *books.*"

"Only if she promises to teach me," I say. I'm not sure

189

where this confidence is coming from, but I'm eating it up. My heart is pounding, but I'm having fun! Maybe this is what my extrovert friends have been talking about all this time. This "socializing" stuff.

"This girl doesn't make promises," she says, looking me up and down. "Especially to a nameless kid she just met."

"Bastian," I say, "Short for Sebastian. Spell it B-A-S-T-I-A-N, but pronounce it however, I'm used to it by now. Pronouns are *he* and *him*. Aquarius sun, Cancer moon, Sagittarius rising—"

"Bastian," she says, cutting me off. "Cool. Still, no promises."

"Come on," I beg. "What if I just want to learn? What if I want to learn how to cook with these because I'm tired of takeout?"

"Count yourself lucky," she says, straightening and folding her arms. "We don't eat it unless we cook it in this house."

"Damn," I say. That's dedication. Must mean her parents are home all the time, then. "Do your parents work?"

"Course," she scoffs, wrinkling her nose, "We all cook over here, not just my parents. Wai— *Why* am I still out here answering your questions?" She grabs the window to close it again.

"Because we're both quarantined," I say, "and bored, stuck at home, with nothing to do but kill time."

"Some of us still have responsibilities," she says.

"Like what, vacuuming? Takes five minutes." I shrug. "Come on, my therapist said I should work on making new friends. You know how hard that is to do in lockdown?"

"You could start by not letting your dog bark at all hours of the night. Y'lose more friends that way."

"Quicker than hucking cats through people's windows?" I say with a laugh. I fold my arms, awkwardly because my arm is still stuck in an L shape.

"Hey, that's a low blow. I apologized for Ruby's behavior . . . and I didn't *huck* her."

"I'm *kidding*," I say. "But that joke was in poor taste. Look, why don't we just start over, huh? I'm sorry for my dog barking so loud over here, and you're sorry for your cat jumping through my window. Fair?"

"You still suck at gardening," she says. I'd assume it's playful but her mouth is completely flat.

"How do you know?" I launch back. I look down at my plants, which I just planted a week ago. "They look fine! Bright green and lush and happy!"

"Just look at your planter box," she says, motioning to it with her chin, "with your 'light-skinned soil-havin' ass."

"Oh, and you can do better?" I ask.

"You *said* I could do better." Oh no, the head wag is out now.

"Did I say you could do better, or did I say they look ready for harvest?" If all else fails in an argument, you can always catch them on a technicality.

"How would you know they're ready for harvest if you don't even cook?"

"You own a cat. Your apartment probably smells like cat. How do *you* know they're ready for harvest if you can't even smell them?"

"Ruby doesn't smell," she growls, but she's wearing a trace of a smile. "Besides, you have a dog. How do *you* smell anything?"

"My dog doesn't pee in the house like a cat!" I tease.

"Well, maybe if he *did*, you wouldn't have to risk your life out here taking him to do his business."

"Actually, my mom takes him for most of the day," I say. I can't help my voice getting a bit softer and sadder. "She . . . drives. People. For money. You know. She, uh . . . got laid off, so this is an in-between thing for her."

There's silence between us, and I can't decide if Billie—so weird that I know her name now!—is processing what I've said or judging me for it. But then she sighs and leans back on the sill again, twiddling her thumbs nervously.

"That sounds dangerous," she says, her voice now calm and soothing, like a healing salve. "Being out like that all day. With the virus and all."

"Yeah," I admit, letting my deep desire to brighten the mood a bit take over. "What about your mom? You said she's out all day too. What's she do?"

"She's an EMT. So she's out all day, especially now."

"Oh."

Definitely didn't lighten the mood much. The awkward silence quickly takes over, and I worry I've gone and mucked this up, royally. Who would want to see a killjoy like me again? I turn my eyes down to my little plants, who despite all the things they must overhear out of me at their place at the windowsill, still don't judge me. *I tried, Mrs. Rosemary,* I think. But then I hear it. Her voice again.

"Tell you what," she says, straightening again. "Since you're right, and I don't have much to do up here, I'll cut you a deal. You have twenty-four hours to prove you're a better gardener than me by giving me *something* that you make with them, and I likewise. We'll have to get creative, with quarantine and all, but if you're really deserving of the 'master gardener' title, you'll find a way. If *I* win, you keep your dog quiet, by any means necessary. Training, or even a muzzle."

"Ouch," I say, wincing in emotional pain. "Just gonna muzzle my best friend like that? Just gonna box in his greatness?"

She nods nonchalantly.

"As long as I'm boxed in across the alley."

"And if I win?" I ask, my heart pounding, wondering what she'll say.

She sighs.

"What are you hoping for?" she asks. "Help with homework?"

"Would you, uh . . ." I balance all my weight on one foot nervously. "Would you think less of me if I asked for your number?"

A car horn beeps just as I say the word *number,* and I worry she didn't hear me right. But then I see red creep into her face, and she doesn't seem to notice her cat walking under her arm and out onto the planter box until it's too late. Reflexively, she grabs at the ball of fluff with claws, just as one of her back paws scoops out a shower of soil and sends it plummeting to the ground.

"Ruby!" she hollers, pulling the cat back through the window despite her incessant meowing. "You know better!"

When Billie pops back through the window again, she takes a long, deep breath.

"Deal."

"Deal?!" I ask happily, hoping I didn't sound thirsty. But the smile she gives me tells me she knows I'm walking the line.

"I said what I said, so now we're even." She smirks. "Almost. Matilda."

Matilda?

"What?" I ask in confusion.

"Billie is short for Matilda. Now you know my real name like I know yours."

I smile, glancing up at the sky and realizing it's getting hazy and warm orange behind the purple clouds. Sunset will be here soon.

"Does that mean you want to see me again?"

"Don't push it, Sebastian." She smiles, leaning back into her apartment and shutting her window. Is it just me, or do her eyes linger on me for just a little longer than I expected before she draws the curtains?

"Yes!" I cry, turning and bolting for my door, sprinting barefoot past Oscar, who's wagging his tail and bouncing around, freaking out, understandably. I scoop him up and let him lick my face.

"Oscar, you gotta help me, boy! We've got a gardening

contest to win! *Mom!*" I holler out to the living room as I hear her keys jingle. Oscar runs to greet her, but I dart down the hall toward the bathroom. "Where is the beeswax?"

"What?" I hear her yell back as I rummage through cabinets of half-empty shampoo bottles and drawers of molds and bottles of oil.

"Where's the beeswax?" I holler louder.

"Top cabinet!"

"Thanks!"

I've got something wonderful to make.

BILLIE VS. LASAGNA

Okay, he may be a little forward, and a little rough around the edges, but when I heard that he has to eat takeout every night . . . like, *every* night? Nobody deserves that. He potentially has never had a homemade lasagna. Just the ready-bake frozen stuff with the wood pulp cheese.

I have to help.

Besides, this is a nice first way to use my new herbs—*all* of them. In fact, I'll make a chicken lasagna, which pairs nicely with the tarragon. I can always garnish with parsley and cilantro, and I'm currently mashing up the basil in my mortar, grinding the pestle against the stone, smearing green along the inside and pressing fragrant scents into the air.

Normally, pesto should sit overnight to let the flavors marry and the olive oil to turn green with basily essence, but if he—Bastian—thinks I'm about to lose a twenty-four-hour challenge over some pity, he's sorely mistaken. Not pity, that's the wrong word. Compassion? That sounds better.

Ruby rubs up on my ankle and meows.

"Come on, Rubles, it's not like that," I insist, tucking a loose curl that slipped out of my puff behind my ear. "He's just a nice kid who deserves some homemade lasagna."

A nice kid who wants your number, comes a voice in my head that I do *not* welcome.

I sigh and roll up my sleeves, because this is hard work.

Okay, *fine.* A nice kid who wants my number. But I won't

have to give it to him if I can just focus on folding this pesto into this shredded chicken, and this mascarpone into these eggs, and layering these pasta sheets between them into one large dish for us, and one miniature ceramic dish for him. Rubles slinks herself between my legs, weaving in and out like she's saying she doesn't believe me.

"Of *course* I want to win, Rubles. Don't be ridiculous," I say. But I keep glancing at the open window, relieved he can't see this far into my apartment so I can cook all of this without an audience, and not really caring if I win or lose. Heat creeps into my cheeks as it sinks in all over again that a nice kid who may not have ever had homemade lasagna . . .

. . . wants my number.

BASTIAN VS. HAND BUTTER

"Oscar, come on," I chide. "Out of the way, this pot is heavy."

And it is, especially since I'm carrying it with only my uncasted arm. It's full of melted cocoa butter and shea butter, after all, which feels like liquid lead. I set it down on the kitchen table in a way that I hope is gentle. It's not. Liquid butter sloshes out of the top and splatters onto the table.

"Oh god," I breathe, slinging newspapers and a sweatshirt I left lying around all over it to wipe it up before it dries and turns into something as stubborn to remove as candle wax. I check my phone time. Four hours left till five p.m., which is the twenty-four-hour deadline. I ladle the butters into the little round flower molds and sprinkle the herbs over the top.

The lavender—my favorite scent—won't be ready for another few weeks. But the others—the sage, the rosemary, and the oregano—are all fragrant and ready to be turned into soap. Or, in this case, bath melts. I gently stir a plastic spoon through the mostly clear liquid, pushing some of the herbs deeper down to distribute the scent evenly.

Oscar lets out a long whine that I can actually hear through the torrent of drums pounding through my headphones, and I slip them off my head and around my shoulders.

"What's up, kiddo?" I ask him. But then I hear what he's freaking out about. A high-pitched, screaming beeping sound like a smoke detector. Except it's not ours. In fact, it sounds like it's coming from outside. Out of curiosity, I set the spoon back in the bowl and make my way over to the window, cracking it open to the incessant beeping that's amplified to an unignorable level. I look across the alley to Billie's window. She's nowhere to be seen, at first, but the lights are clearly on. Then, suddenly, Billie appears behind the glass in a flash and flings open the window, releasing a gentle haze of smoke out into the evening air.

"You okay?" I call up to her, but I don't think she hears me, because she immediately turns to address whatever's burning in there. Oscar looks up at me from the cushion to my left.

"It's okay, buddy," I say, fluffing his fur. "I'm sure she's fine, whatever she's making in there."

But as I turn to leave, Oscar barks at me, beckoning me back to the window.

"What, you want me to just stare up there like a weirdo? She already caught me staring before. I don't want to make her uncomfortable."

He barks again.

"Of course a dog would tell me to do that. Y'all be sniffin' each other's butts and stuff."

He whines.

"You know I didn't mean it like that. It's just a fact, okay? I'm sure she's fine. Besides, I've gotta get these in the fridge so they can set."

I take the pan and slide it into the fridge, realizing that I never figured out a way to get this to her. With the pandemic, this is feeling a little implausible. Couldn't we have just met at the window at five and waxed poetic about how wonderful our own concoctions are?

Nah, I think, *not my style.*

Pandemic or not, quarantine or not, I've got to find a way to get this to her.

In person.

BILLIE VS. THE SWAP

I knew I should've taken up juggling instead.

This gardening hobby got me creeping out the front door of our apartment cradling a baking dish of lasagna under my arm like a masked, hooded Black Santa Claus, just so I can prove I'm the better gardener, which should be obvious at this point. I've spent three weeks reading books on soil types, ideal sunlight and water conditions, and everything else a good plant parent should do. I've got this.

I sanitized the outside of the container, lid and all, so I smell like sanitizer and tomato sauce. But the air out here smells fresh and clear. On days like today, I'm glad I live in the Pacific Northwest, surrounded by mountains and trees in the distance, which share their fresh air with us, even deep in the city. I turn and walk to the next building over—the complex where Bastian lives.

"Hi," I say to the front desk woman, who's wearing a mask and surrounded by all kinds of sanitation wipes, sprays, cloths, extra masks, and hand sanitizer. Without a word, she picks up the latter and holds it out to me. Since I'm holding the tray of lasagna, I set it gently on the counter and use the sanitizer, even though I'm going back out the front door in about twenty seconds.

"I, um," I begin. How do I explain that I'm leaving this lasagna for a resident whose apartment number I don't know, whose last name I don't know, and who I've technically never met in person? I clear my throat and try to organize my thoughts. "I made this for a resident—"

"Name?"

"Billie," I answer, and then realize she may be asking for *his* name. "Oh, uh, his name is Bastian. Sebastian."

She looks up at me now, her blue eyes weighed down by her dark, thick eyebrows. "The takeout kid."

A pang of sadness and shock hits me. The *takeout* kid? Does she commonly refer to residents by how much food they have to order because they may not know how to cook for themselves?

"Yeah," I say, unable to hide my disgust.

"He's been a bit quiet lately. Thought he mighta got the virus."

My heart skips. What a callous, cruel thing to say. This virus may be everywhere, but Mom comes home with horror stories of the symptoms every day. Visions of ever-weakening patients with lung lacerations dance in my head, and I swallow at the thought of Bastian joining them. I begin to wonder if I've sanitized the baking dish enough.

"Could I have one of your wipes, please?" I ask. She hands me the wipes, and once I've resanitized the dish—lid, underside, and especially the handles—I toss the wipe in the trash and nod goodbye to the attendant.

"It's hot, so if you have any way to call him down . . . I just don't want it to get cold."

And just like that, I realize he's gone from being "the boy next door with the obnoxiously loud dog" to "the boy next door who I'd venture outside for during quarantine, just to make sure he has a hot home-cooked meal."

And the fact that my chest is pounding as I ascend the stairs back to my own apartment, and that I'm running through the list of ingredients I used—did I add enough salt? Did I garnish with too much cilantro? Did I let the mozzarella on top brown enough? As if I haven't made homemade lasagna a thousand times—tells me . . . *something*.

Something's changed.

BASTIAN VS. THE GAP

I forgot the apartment building next door is the *fancy* one—the one you need a passcode to get into just to speak to the front desk. So here I am, walking back to my own complex with these sloppily molded hand butter melts in this ugly paper bag, wondering how in the world I'm going to get them to her. I check my phone and realize I have fourteen minutes to get these into her apartment before I lose the contest. And then, why would she give me her number?

I'm loud. She knows I don't read. I like dogs, she likes cats. I don't cook. She thinks I've been watching her through her window. That's six strikes.

Blow this shot, and I'm out, I know it.

So I run back through my complex's lobby, but Gail, the front desk person, calls for me.

"Bastian, hey! You got something here."

"Yeah?" I ask.

Because Gail was uber-paranoid about germs *before* the virus, she's triple extra uber-paranoid now that quarantine is in full force. After pulling out two wipes, one for each hand, she uses them to lift up a white round baking dish as big across as my hand. I catch a faint whiff of tomato sauce.

"What . . ." I begin, not understanding, "What's that? Is it for me?"

"Some girl left it a few minutes ago. Said it should be eaten hot. She didn't look like a delivery person. I don't know what it is. Eat it at your own risk."

I lift the lid and smell, taking in the scent of basil, cilantro, meat, and tomato sauce. I close my eyes and fully bask in the best thing I've ever smelled. This is no frozen lasagna. This is the real deal. I take the dish in my arms carefully, avoiding my left arm so I don't melt my cast, cradling it like it's a newborn baby.

"Thanks, Gail. Really. Thank you."

My stomach growls greedily as I ascend the stairs, and I can't wait to get to my room to fully enjoy it. But first, I have to find a way to get this paper bag through that window. And then it hits me.

That's it!

"Hey!" I call out after flinging open my window and waving. She's exchanged her sweatshirt for a loose white T-shirt that ties in the front. Same bell-shaped hair, same big brown eyes, same comfortable, curled-up position she sits in by the window. She sees me and opens the glass.

"You admitting defeat?" she asks as I hold up the baking dish.

"Just from the smell alone, I probably should," I admit. "It's already amazing."

"Taste it!" she urges. Her face seems brighter today, glowier. I know that look anywhere. It's the look of someone immersed in their passion. Maybe cooking is hers like aromatherapy is mine.

"So," I say, "before I get to your gift—"

"Whoa, whoa," she says, "Not a gift. A *contest entry*. We're still competitors, don't you forget."

I grin.

"Stubborn, are we? Okay, 'contest entry.' I have to get you mine. I couldn't get through the front door, but I'd say I should have clearance to toss this bad boy through your window like your cat jumped through mine."

She laughs.

"Seriously? Weak."

"Hey, you want me to enter this contest or not?"

"I don't know if I trust your throwing skills," she says.

"Got a better idea?" I ask.

She hesitates for a moment. I don't want to admit that I'm hoping she says she'll meet me at her front door, but . . . I am. But I'm also not, because deodorant has been a thing of the past since I've been home all day, and there's *no* way I'm meeting her smelling like . . . like this.

"Catch," I say, leaning out the window holding it in my hand. She leans forward with arms extended and says, "Fine, but toss at your own risk. If you miss, you're out."

Believe me, I know.

My forehead is dotted with sweat, and my hands are clammy.

But I fling the bag, aiming at her planter box, and it goes sailing through the space between us, closing the gap. Everything seems to happen in slow motion. It spins in the air as it sails toward her.

BILLIE VS. THE BAG

I reach out, still in disbelief that this kid just *tossed* me his contest entry. Either he really doesn't care if he gets my number, or he has a lot of faith in his tossing—and my catching—ability. The bag hits my fingertips and bounces off, and my spirit drops, but I lean farther out the window, farther than I'm comfortable, to reach for the bag.

BASTIAN VS. DISBELIEF

———

I stare in disbelief at this girl, who's gone from being the annoyed kid across the alley who keeps calling the front desk to complain about my dog, to the girl who's about to fall out a window to catch something I made for her.

BILLIE VS. DISORIENTATION

I can't believe I almost fell out a window for a boy I just met.

But here I am, staring down at him with one hand cradled under the bundle he threw to me, and the other hand clamped around the edge of my window, holding me inside the building. Ruby walks over the bay window cushion, meowing her *I told you so*—I'm sure that's what she said in cat-speak. I clear my throat, curl up next to the window, and catch my breath. He's still sitting there by his window, chin on his fists, staring at me with the lasagna dish between his elbows, lost in thought.

"Hey," I say, holding up the paper-bag-wrapped gift in my hand. It feels like something hard is inside. Maybe gumballs? Strangely shaped gumballs? "Swap on the count of three?"

As if I've caught him daydreaming—and I might have—he startles and pulls the lid off his lasagna. I can see the steam rising from here.

"Smells good, gotta say," he says. "Knew that was basil." And before I can even get my bag open, he's spooning the first bite into his mouth. He shuts his eyes, leans his head back, hands up in surrender.

"You win," he says. "No contest. I give up. This is bomb. You sure you didn't order this straight from Italy?"

"That mean you don't want my number after all?" I ask,

reaching into the bag and pulling out . . . "What are these, cookies?"

My tongue brushes the cookie just as I hear his "No, don't—!"

I cough, recognizing the combinations of smells right away. It smelled so much like shortbread, I thought it might be. But no. Just shea butter. Fresh herbs. And what smells like cocoa butter too.

"I agree, this tastes terrible." I cough. "You lose."

"It's hand butter!" He laughs. "Y'all don't read labels over there?"

I roll my eyes and look into the bag. One, two, three, four, five, six hand butter bars shaped like flowers, and one small white square of paper. I pull it out and read the careful handwriting.

I think you're beautiful. And cool. And I have a surprise for you. Text me?

And there's a phone number listed below.

"Sneaky," I say, smirking at him.

"Doesn't sound like a no," he says, hands up, before spooning another generous helping of lasagna into his mouth.

"We'll see," I say, smoothing one of the flowers over my hands. The oregano scent comes through against the cocoa butter, making these smell like herbaceous sugar cookies. With everything that's happened, I know I could use a friend.

But I like a tease.

So I leave him with one last smile before closing the window gently, and I turn to my room. My hands are shaking and sweaty. I take a long deep breath and crawl under the covers—back to my safe place. And then I do something I hope my therapist would be proud of me for.

I text him.

Me: You win.

Him: <3

My whole face goes hot at a single emoji. *Really, girl?* I ask myself, rolling my eyes at my own softness. But two more texts come through that make me even more shy. A screenshot, and an invitation. *Pacific Northwest Fall Herb Festival. Tickets limited. Learn to cook with herbs fresh and dried. Food, drinks, and aromatherapy.*

Him: Thought we could learn to cook together.

I don't recognize this boldness I feel bubbling from me, but I love it. I go and find the link to my grandmother's lasagna recipe from my mother's blog and send it to him with the caption:

Me: Why wait?

Stuck with Her

by Rachael Lippincott

I think I might have discovered another circle of Hell: Quarantining with your horrible, messy, way-too-loud, *way-too-obnoxious* roommate, who thinks the middle of the night is the perfect time to blast a Spotify playlist.

We've been roommates since she answered my Facebook post about needing one after my sophomore year on-campus housing fell through this past summer. I remember clicking through all of her pictures, thinking she looked normal. Nice. Pretty, even.

I could not have been more wrong. Well . . . not about the pretty thing, but literally *everything* else. She's been the very definition of annoying since move-in day, from dishes left piled in the sink to using up all the hot water in the shower.

Aside from just our daily spats between classes over stolen

food and taking out the trash, her friends give her some pretty strong competition for the top slot of Most Irritating, as they join her in obliterating our living room every Saturday night. I joined them *once* and left after half an hour, covered in Tom Allen's heaping plate of chips and queso after he drunkenly tripped over his own two feet.

I guess that's one good thing about quarantine. My living room is still intact come Sunday morning.

Groaning, I grab my pillow and press it down over my head, trying to block out the music that's blaring its way into my room from the kitchen.

Or trying to smother myself. Either would be a solution.

I squeeze my eyes shut and turn onto my right side. Then my left. Then my back. But it's no use. The steady bass still manages to make its way through, bopping any chance I have of completing another REM cycle right out the window.

Ripping the pillow away from my face, I fumble around on my bedside table for my phone, the screen lighting up with a tap of my thumb. I squint at the glaring numbers, my rage nearing a rolling boil as *3:03* comes swinging into focus.

I . . . am going to kill her.

I roll out of bed and jam my feet into my slippers before angrily wrestling with a hoodie, my arms getting tangled somewhere between the neck and armholes, the congestive fleece upping my frustration tenfold.

Yanking open my bedroom door, I storm across the living room, turn into the kitchen, and make a beeline for the black Bluetooth speaker on the wobbly, Craigslist-bought kitchen table. My first instinct is to launch the speaker across the room, but I opt for just flicking the power button off, the song cutting sharply off into silence.

Finally.

I spin around to see Mia lounging on the counter, elbow deep in a bag of *my* Doritos, her long, dark hair pulled into a messy bun. She stops chewing and holds the bag out to me, her fingers coated in bright orange dust. "Dorito?"

I roll my eyes and snatch the bag out of her hand.

"Seriously, Mia? What about now seems like a good time to start playing music?" I say as I roll the crinkly red bag back up, slamming it back onto *my* side of the snack shelf.

She swings her legs, calves hitting the cabinet underneath her. "I dunno. Got done with studying and the apartment seemed a little quiet."

"That's because it is three o'clock. In the *morning*. It's *supposed* to be quiet."

I watch as she smirks and hops down off the counter, her cool blue eyes giving me an amused once-over. "Why? You got somewhere to be tomorrow?"

I glare at her. "For your information, I have *two* Zoom classes."

"*Two Zoom classes,*" she mimics, reaching out to tug at the two heather gray drawstrings of my sweatshirt until they're perfectly even. The close proximity startles me for a second. Maybe two. Finally, I swat her hand away, my heart hammering angrily in my chest. "You do know you can just like . . . turn your camera off and sleep during those."

"How are you not failing out of school? Isn't your major molecular biology?"

"Because I stay up at night to study," she says, motioning to the room around us, the edge of her right hand stained blue from her after-hours note taking. "Obviously."

"Well, maybe if you studied during—"

She lets out a big, dramatic yawn, stretching loudly, the noise cutting me off midsentence. "Sorry, Allie. You know how much I love chatting with you, but I am just *exhausted,*" she says, like *I'm* the one keeping *her* up. "Think I'm gonna head to bed."

You have got to be kidding me.

She slides past me and I watch as she saunters off down the hallway to her room, the very picture of innocence.

I stand there in shock, too angry to form a coherent sentence.

"You—I . . ."

"Night!" she calls from her doorway, giving me one more infuriating smirk before flicking on the light and disappearing inside.

"Stop eating my Doritos!" I manage to get out before the door clicks shut behind her.

Stop eating my Doritos. Really?

"That's the best you could come up with, Allie?" I mutter to myself as I stomp back across the living room to my bedroom, determined to get at least a few more hours of sleep.

And to work on my comebacks.

215

—

I wake up the next morning feeling like crap.

My alarm blares noisily next to me for the fourth time, my phone tangled somewhere in my striped sheets. Flopping onto my side with a frustrated groan, I dig around to find it, the sound cutting out with a tap of the stop button. Even though my first Zoom class of the day is only ten minutes away, I burrow back into my warm comforter, wrapping myself up like a burrito. My eyes land on a Polaroid picture of my fluffy brown rescue dog, Jericho, his tongue lolling out as he keeps watch over the neighborhood from the front steps of my childhood home.

A sharp pain radiates across my chest, a wave of sadness and anxiety crashing into me as I stare at the familiar red brick house and worn black shutters just behind his squirrelly little head. Just like I've been doing for the past couple months, I push the unwanted feelings as far down as I can manage, and then flail out of my covers, angrily de-burritoing myself as I swing my legs over the side of my bed.

I set up my laptop and go to the bathroom before zipping into the kitchen to grab a bowl of cereal, the clock ticking closer and closer to class time. As I'm shutting the refrigerator door, I catch sight of the speaker on the counter.

I stick my head out of the kitchen to peer down the hall at Mia's closed door before tiptoeing over to it. Flipping it over, I claw at the black battery cover, trying for a solid thirty seconds to get it to open.

"Come on . . ." I mutter, wincing as I nearly break a nail off, the tiny plastic door flying through the air and clattering noisily on the counter.

I smile to myself as I grab the two double-A batteries, pocket them, and quickly return the cover to the back of the—

"Morning," a voice says from behind me.

I jump about a mile and whip around to see Mia opening a crinkly silver Pop-Tart wrapper, her chestnut-brown hair pulled into a low ponytail. "Oh, hi! Morning!" I say, *way* more chipper and friendly than I ever have to her.

She slowly takes a bite of the brown sugar cinnamon Pop-Tart in her hand, narrowing her eyes suspiciously at me.

"I, uh . . ." My eyes dart down to the cereal bowl on the counter. I walk quickly over and scoop it up, walking backward out of the kitchen. "I gotta go . . . I have class . . . Zoom class . . ."

She raises one of her eyebrows at me as I scurry off to my room, slamming the door behind me.

"Could you *be* any more suspicious?" I mumble as I plunk into my swivel chair.

Class has already started by the time I realize I forgot to get a spoon.

And that Mia was eating one of my Pop-Tarts.

—

I wish I could say that taking the batteries out put an end to her middle-of-the-night kitchen DJing, but it absolutely did not. I do it every single morning for a week, a small pile form-ing in my top desk drawer, but it doesn't make a difference.

I *still* get woken up at three in the freaking morning to the sound of overly autotuned vocals and a beat that belongs firmly in the club, not in my apartment *hours* before sunrise.

And every night, I storm out to see Mia, apparent owner of a lifetime supply of double-A batteries, lounging on the counter, swaying to the music, and eating *my* food.

Two nights ago, it was handfuls of popcorn. Yesterday, she was picking all of the marshmallows out of my Lucky Charms like an actual psychopath.

Which is maybe why tonight . . . I can't even get to sleep. I toss and turn for hours, jolting awake every time I drift off, my heart hammering in my chest, my sheets wrapped tightly around my body.

Feeling trapped, I push my covers off and stare around at the dark room, my eyes landing on the Polaroid picture. I can barely make out the red brick house behind it.

Sighing, I climb out of bed and go over to the window, the light from the street lamps just outside bathing my skin in a warm yellow glow.

Everything on the other side of the glass is eerily quiet and still, even for this time of night. Not a single car passes by. Not a single person walking on the street.

I peer across the way, to another apartment building, and find some comfort in the flicker of a TV screen, a few stray lights on, but the anxiety still claws at my chest.

How long will I be stuck in here?

How long will the world be like *this*? Without any clear future, the "normal" of a few weeks ago impossible to go back to.

I didn't even *like* going out that much, but I'd kill to set foot in a coffee shop. Or a bookstore. Or even go to the movies. Heck, I'd even splurge and spend a week's worth of grocery money on an overpriced popcorn drenched in butter and a soda that's mostly ice.

I wonder when it will even be safe to *go* to a movie theater again? Or a *concert*? Or a—

Like Mia can sense my inner turmoil, I hear the music begin to blare from the kitchen. The singer has barely started singing before I bust out of my room, skid around the corner into the kitchen, and grab the speaker, poised to smash it into a hundred pieces.

"Whoa, whoa, whoa," Mia says, her blue eyes wide, her hands outstretched like she's just come across a rabid squirrel and wants it to know she means no harm. "Allie. *Put the speaker down.*"

I hesitate, holding it over my head for a second before slamming it down on the kitchen table between us, the music cutting out abruptly. "Then stop playing music at three in the morning, Mia! *Jesus,* do you have an unlimited supply of batteries or something?"

My hands wrap around the wooden chair in front of me. "I am *tired.* I am tired of being woken up every single night. I am tired of taking classes online, and not being able to go outside, and not knowing when things will be okay again. And I'm tired of being stuck in this stupid apartment with *you.*"

She throws her hands up, exasperated. "Well, if you hate me so much, you should've just gone home to quarantine. I mean, you've been miserable since you came back from Christmas break. I thought you'd jump at the opportunity to get out of here."

Home. The red brick house, Jericho on the front steps. The exact thing I've been trying not to think about.

The word instantly sends my heart rate into triple time, my chest constricting, the panic attack I've felt haunting every waking moment for the last three weeks of lockdown finally blindsiding me. I take an unsteady step back and reach out to grab the wall.

Mia's demeanor instantly changes. Her blue eyes study my face, her dark eyebrows furrowing as she steps around the kitchen table, moving closer to me.

"Hey, Allie . . ."

I turn on my heel, folding my arms tightly across my chest, trying to contain it . . . trying to keep it in . . . but it's no use. I start to shake, my teeth chattering as I pace back and forth across the living room, everything too raw. Too bright.

You're okay.

Everything is okay.

I register Mia in the doorway of the kitchen, her face filled with concern.

"Talk to me," I manage to get out, my breathing coming out in staggered gasps, the white walls closing in as I walk back and forth across the hardwood floor. Back and forth.

"Um. What's your favorite color?"

"Yellow," I say as my eyes jump around the room. Faded carpet. Lamp. Striped socks. Hole in the toe.

"Birthday?"

"October twenty-third."

"Coffee or tea?"

"Uh," I spin around on my heel. Flat-screen TV. Worn gray couch. White Converse by the door. "Iced coffee, hot tea."

I pull at the collar of my oversized T-shirt, and Mia strides over to the window, yanking it open, the cool air drifting across the room. I go over and slide down on the wall underneath it, the wind tugging at the top of my head, strands of my blond hair whipping around my face. Mia sits down next to me, a few inches away, her hand resting on the worn wood in-between us.

Something about her being so close calms me.

Reflexively, I reach out, my fingertips sliding into the palm of her hand, the skin smooth and warm and comforting.

"What's your favorite season?" she asks as our fingers intertwine, grounding me.

"Fall. I like when the leaves change."

"Same," Mia says, her thumb softly tracing circles against my pointer finger, around and around, over and over again. "Favorite movie?"

"*Booksmart.*"

I squeeze my eyes shut, a jumble of scenes from the movie dancing behind my eyelids as I try to focus on my breathing without accidentally causing myself to hyperventilate. I count silently in my head as my lungs rise and fall.

Four in. Hold for seven. Eight out.

Four in. Hold for seven. Eight out.

I can feel the panic slowly begin to fade, becoming more and more manageable with every exhale, the tightness and pressure in my chest and head gradually starting to release its grip.

"Which of my friends do you hate the most?"

I *almost* crack a smile at that, a backward baseball cap and brown eyes popping into my head. "Tom."

"Queso incident?"

I nod my confirmation. "Queso incident."

"That's fair," she says, stifling a laugh before continuing. "Coolest place you've ever traveled to?"

"Grand Canyon. We went for my seventh birthday. It was . . . unreal."

"Favorite food?"

"The pizza at Mario's on 13th Street. They have two-dollar, two-slice Tuesdays. It's to die for."

"Aren't you lactose intolerant?" Mia asks.

I open my eyes and turn my head to look over at her, surprised she knows this random bit of trivia about me. "Well . . . I said it was to die for."

She smiles at that. A real smile. Not one of her passive-aggressive, midfight smirks that makes my blood boil.

It lights up her whole face, her blue eyes brighter than I've ever seen them, a dimple I've never noticed before appearing on her right cheek.

"Mario's is pretty good, but there's a pizza place back where I'm from that makes a *mean* Hawaiian pizza."

I grimace. "You would be the kind of person to like pineapple on pizza."

"Guilty as charged," she says, not one-upping me for once. I watch as she looks away, tilting her head back to rest on the wall behind us.

I take one more slow breath in and hold it, my eyes registering the straight line of Mia's nose, the fullness of her lips.

When I let the air go, I finally feel back in control of my body.

"This is . . . so crazy."

"What?" Mia asks. "Us actually having a peaceful conversation?"

I laugh, nudging her arm lightly. "*That*. But also everything happening in the world right now. Quarantine. The coronavirus."

"Murder hornets," Mia adds.

I nod. "Some days it feels like the freaking apocalypse."

"What a way to go. Holed up in an apartment, stuffing ourselves with Pop-Tarts and cereal."

"Stuffing ourselves with *my* Pop-Tarts and cereal," I correct.

Mia grins at that, the dimple reappearing. "Stuffing ourselves with *your* Pop-Tarts and cereal," she echoes.

We both fall silent and I realize I'm still holding her hand, her fingers folded gently over mine.

I notice a thin scar running from the base of her pointer finger all the way down to her thumb, the raised, pale skin standing out against the olive of the rest of her hand.

"What happened?" I ask, nodding to it.

Mia glances down, tilting our hands to get a better look at the scar. "Nothing interesting." She chuckles to herself, shaking her head. "When I was a kid, one of my older brothers ran over it with his bike and shattered three different bones. I had to get surgery and everything."

I grimace at the mental image of that. "How many brothers do you have?"

"Four. And three sisters. I've got a pretty big family." Our eyes meet and she shrugs, the corner of her mouth ticking up into a soft smile. "That's partly why I play music at night. Too much quiet kind of freaks me out."

"What's the other part?"

"Annoying you. Obviously."

I roll my eyes and swat at her shoulder. She laughs, dodging out of the way, seven siblings' worth of practice behind her.

"You must miss them," I say, and her face grows a little more serious, her eyebrows jutting down.

"At least half of them," she jokes, but the light doesn't fully meet her eyes. There's definitely a lingering sadness there.

"Why didn't you go home?" I ask.

"I couldn't." She sits up a little straighter and lets out a long exhale. "A last-minute, cross-country plane ticket was *way* too expensive. I would've had to sell at *least* one kidney to pay for it."

She doesn't ask why I can't go home, but I find myself wanting to tell her, wanting someone to share the weight of it for just a little while.

I take a deep breath, the words I've been holding back for

months tumbling out. "My parents pretty much disowned me over Christmas break."

Mia's eyes widen in surprise, and she turns to look at me.

"They're, uh." I look away, swallowing. "They're super religious. Always have been. Church-every-Sunday, hosting-Bible-study-on-Fridays, Harry-Potter-is-blasphemy kind of religious." I laugh, thinking back to a random retreat I went on my freshman year of high school where we had a two-hour-long sermon on the sanctity of marriage and the horrors of premarital sex. "I even signed an abstinence pledge when I was *fourteen*, which is the Catholic school version of sex ed."

Mia doesn't laugh at that. She just watches me, her expression concerned.

"Anyway, I came out to them on the last day of break, and they pretty much told me to never come back because I'm, you know . . . a massive disappointment who's going against God's plan for my life." I squint, trying to keep it together. "Which, I mean, I *knew* they'd say. I even packed my bags before telling them because I knew they weren't going to be okay with it."

My voice cracks on the last word and I swallow, my vision blurring as tears begin to stream down my face. What a terrible price to pay, just so I can be fully and completely and honestly myself.

"I just think maybe I secretly hoped they would find a way to be okay with it, you know? Okay with *me*."

A sob escapes my lips and Mia's instantly there, her arms wrapping around me, as the panic and the hurt and the sadness

I've forced down for *months* finds its way to the surface, the pressure of quarantine squeezing it out.

I don't know how long we sit there for.

Me, crying like an actual baby, definitely getting snot on her black sweatshirt.

Mia, gently rubbing my back through all of it, her black, snot-covered sweatshirt smelling like the vial of sandalwood perfume in our bathroom cabinet, warm and woody and comforting.

Soon, the tears start to slow, a heavy tiredness setting in as two thoughts crystallize in my mind.

The first thought is that, deep in my bones, I know I'm going to be okay. It may hurt for a while—in fact, it will probably always hurt, some days and moments more than others—but I'll survive. This isn't going to break me or change who I know I am.

And . . . the second thought is, as her arms tighten around me, my eyelids slowly closing, that . . . I don't hate it. I don't hate sitting here, my face pressed into Mia's warm, sandalwood-smelling shoulder. I don't hate the way her hand feels in mine, and the way she always knows, good or bad, exactly what to say.

I don't hate *her*.

—

I wake up the next morning on the hardwood floor underneath the open window, a fleece blanket over me, and one of the lumpy pillows from the couch tucked under my head.

I feel something on my forehead, and frown, peeling off a fluorescent pink sticky note and squinting at the loopy cursive.

Couldn't wake you up. Gone to get groceries. (Shocking, I know). Be back in a bit.—M

I smile at the tiny *M,* rubbing the spot on my forehead where the sticky note had been, last night washing back over me, my stomach fluttering with butterflies as I think about . . .

Beep, beep, beep!

I rip the fleece blanket off, fumbling around until I find my phone, the screen lighting up to show my 10:05 a.m., *YOU'RE LATE FOR CLASS* alarm.

Oh crap. I jump up, the butterflies floating straight out the open window as my back splinters into a thousand pieces, a night of sleeping on the floor taking its toll.

Throwing the blanket and the pillows back on the couch, I limp-run into my room, closing the door behind me and sliding into my desk chair. I manage to log in before the actual lesson starts, saved by my Calculus II teacher wrestling with technological difficulties and slow Wi-Fi.

I try to pay attention and take notes, but I find myself distracted by every little noise on the other side of the door, my head swimming with thoughts of Mia.

About halfway through the lesson on parametric equations, I finally hear her come back, the front door creaking open, the sound of her feet shuffling back and forth across the floor as she sanitizes everything in the hallway before bringing it inside.

I pull my eyes away from my professor's face, holding my

breath and listening as she moves, from the entryway, to the kitchen, and then eventually back to her room, the door closing behind her as my heart dances noisily around inside my chest.

I'm so deep in thought I barely realize when class ends. And even after it's over, I don't budge from my seat.

In fact, I hide in my room for most of the day, trying, and failing, to study for my Art History exam on Monday, my new and unexpected feelings much easier to deal with when I don't have to see that smug smirk and those cool blue eyes and the newly discovered dimple on her right cheek that appears only when she smiles.

Sighing, I pull open my desk drawer and stare at the pile of double-A batteries sitting at the bottom.

I roll my eyes and lean back in my chair. *Get ahold of yourself, Allie.*

Never in a million years would I have predicted this. A *crush*. On Mia. Infuriating, annoying, keeps-me-up-all-night Mia.

But I can't help but feel like . . . something shifted between us last night. All of our months of head-butting and frustration and animosity changed shape into something else entirely.

For me, at least.

Does she . . . could she . . . feel the same way?

I groan, in part because my back decides to hit me with an alarmingly painful post-floor-sleep twinge, and in part because I am stuck in an apartment for the foreseeable future with a girl I thought I despised, but really like a whole heck of a lot.

—

My room is still dark when I wake up.

Rubbing my eyes, I reach out for my phone, the illuminated screen blaring out *2:53,* only minutes before Mia's usual middle-of-the-night, post-studying kitchen pop concert.

I roll over on my side and stare at the faint light trickling into my room from underneath the door frame, my ears straining for the familiar music that's blared its way across our apartment every night for over a week.

I wait and I listen, tossing and turning.

3:00 comes and goes. 3:05. Then 3:10.

Soon, it's almost a quarter past, and there's still nothing. Only an ear-ringing silence.

Is she awake?

Curiosity gets the better of me, and I pull back my covers and get out of bed, padding across the floor to my bedroom door.

I pull it open, peeking outside to see that the kitchen light is on. Creeping across the living room, I pop my head around the corner to see Mia in a staring contest with the toaster oven, two slices of cinnamon raisin bread getting steadily crispier on the other side of the glass.

My stomach flip-flops at the sight of her.

She's humming away, a pair of white earbuds sticking out of her ears, the cord looping its way down to her cellphone, tucked safely into her back pocket.

A pair of *earbuds?*

You've got to be kidding me.

I storm across the kitchen and pull the left one out of her ear, shaking my head in disbelief. "Mia. You've had these this *entire* time?"

She jumps in surprise at my sudden and *very* unexpected appearance.

"Jesus, Allie," she says, clutching at her chest. "It is *three* in the morning. You can't just sneak up on someone like that."

"You didn't answer my question."

"Uh . . . yeah," she says, her eyes flicking down to the earbud in my hand, and then back up to meet my glower.

"And you didn't use them because. . . . ?"

"Because if I'd used them you wouldn't have come out here to yell at me every single night." She leans closer and grabs the earbud back from me, the corner of her mouth ticking up into that familiar smirk of hers. A smirk that's more charming than infuriating now, the dimple on her right cheek appearing as it transforms into a smile.

I roll my eyes, but I can't help but smile back, something about her words making me feel the tiniest bit hopeful.

"Why would you want me to come out here and yell at you every single night?"

"Well . . ." She swallows, her voice trailing off. "Well, with quarantine and all, you're pretty much the only person I see. And you're in your room most of the time, so, you know . . . it can get kind of lonely."

I nod, the twinge of hope from a moment ago snuffed out in an instant.

She turns her attention back to the toaster to watch the cinnamon raisin bread. We're both silent for a long moment, staring at our reflections in the tiny glass door.

"Also, it doesn't hurt that I've been harboring a bit of a crush on you since move-in day."

A *what*?

I whip my head around to look at her. "Since move-in day? *Move-in day*, Mia?"

She grins and glances over at me, knowing exactly what's coming.

"You literally *broke* the elevator on move-in day. I had to carry all my stuff up the stairs."

"I didn't *break* the elevator, Allie. It's not my fault that thing is ancient! I held one button for a little bit too long, and the entire elevator shorted out," she says, throwing her hands in the air. "How was I supposed to know that was going to happen?"

"There was a *sign*! Literally *right* above it."

"In like eight-point font!"

"Oh my *God*, you are so annoying," I say as I squeeze my eyes shut, rubbing them. "Why do I even like you?"

I freeze, the both of us realizing what I just said.

I slowly open my fingers to see Mia's cool blue eyes, one of her eyebrows raised, that charming, infuriating, blood-boiling smirk plastered on her face. "You what?"

I pull my hands away. "Oh, don't smirk at me, Mia. You think because I—"

She kisses me, her lips cutting me off midsentence. It's

quick, and sweet, and sends the entire room spinning, my legs and my arms turning into Jell-O as her hands find my waist.

We pull apart and she smiles at me, that dimple on her right cheek appearing.

"You know," I say, reaching up to lightly touch her cheek. "I don't think I'd want to be stuck in an apartment during a global pandemic with anyone else."

If someone had told me a week ago I'd be saying that, I'd have called them crazy.

Mostly because there was a hidden truth that I had refused to ever acknowledge.

Behind every fight, and every sleepless night, and every marshmallow stolen out of my Lucky Charms box, there was something more. There was me *wanting* to talk to her, and me *wanting* to be around her, and me not really caring if she ate all the food on my half of the snack shelf, as long as she had something to eat.

And as long as I could annoy her about it after.

"Me neither," Mia says.

The toaster dings, but she ignores it, pulling me closer. She kisses me again, that spark that used to fuel every argument we've ever had finding a new home, as the room around us disappears.

Masked

by Erin Hahn

GRAY

In a world of Bing Crosbys, my perfect guy would probably be a Danny Kaye. Sweet-talking, talented dancer, gangly limbs and a smile that radiates pure sunshine. To me, Danny Kaye is the epitome of 1950s classic cinema charm. You can keep Bing's smooth baritone and polish. I don't want it.

However, I might be convinced to change my stance, if only for Rosemary Clooney's dress in the "Love, You Didn't Do Right by Me" number in *White Christmas.*

That's how much I love that dress.

Gray: I'd give up Danny Kaye for that dress.

Jude: Whoa.

Jude: Bold words.

I giggle as I read his reply, turning up the volume on my laptop to fully appreciate Clooney's song. Halfway through the scene, my A2NeighborGram tab flashes again, and I click on it.

Jude: Thankfully, you're a genius with a needle, so you can have both!

I sigh, my cursor hovering over Jude's avatar, a tiny black-and-white photo of Danny Kaye's headshot that he put up as a joke after the first time we chatted. I'm pretty sure Jude and I are the only two people under age forty-five on this app, not to mention the only ones not paying a mortgage. It's supposed to be used as a tool for communication around the various neighborhoods in Ann Arbor, Michigan. You know, lost dogs and lawn-mowing services and the like. But last week I put up an ad for face masks, and Jude happened to be scrolling for his uncle's pandemic-ready, porch-to-porch delivery business, and we've been chatting ever since.

Gray: Contrary to what Hallmark would have you believe, Christmas movies aren't real life. Danny Kaye wasn't an immortal, and worldwide pandemics wait for no prom.

Jude: . . .

You see, I've been sewing ever since my grandma gave me her prized Singer and taught me how to hem my first Halloween costume. While some kids were actively auditioning for lead roles in children's summer theater camp, I was the only one begging to apprentice in costume design. *The Wizard of Oz, Les Misérables, Oklahoma!* . . . I've seen it and done it. I rarely have time to make things for myself, and honestly, when would I wear one of my fancy creations?

Which is all to say, I've been planning my prom dress for years. From the moment I saw Rosemary Clooney step onstage in that black gown and shimmery gloves, I was head over heels. I couldn't wait to have curves worthy of a gown like that. I practiced the scalloped neckline the entire summer before my senior year. I saved the money I made doing bridesmaid dress alterations for the expensive fabric.

But then Mr. COVID-19 came to town.

Jude: Are you sure you don't want to save your dress?

Jude: My uncle has material. People have been donating scraps.

The truth is, I thought about saving my dress and maybe using it for a college formal or a wedding or something, but even still, it was so fancy. Too fancy for anything less than prom. I spent a solid four days pouting and raging and making my family as miserable as I was, until I got a call from my aunt Cam. She works as a special events coordinator in a nursing home, where they were out of face masks. The nurses and doctors were the front-line workers who needed the real-deal PPE, but the rest of the nursing home staff needed something to make sure they wouldn't get their patients or their families sick. Cam was a wreck over it.

So I cut into the spare material I'd been saving for the scalloped back panel of my dress and made seven reusable masks. I put them in the mail that night. I figured I wasn't using the scraps. It was being wasted in my room, along with my talent for sewing.

She liked them so much, she asked if I could make a few more. For the nighttime staff, she said.

I was out of scraps, so I cut into the mermaid-fit skirt that originally gathered at my knees and swooped and swished along the floor. I could make it into a modified tea length, I thought, and that mermaid skirt had a whole ton of gathers. Plenty of material to share. It made twenty more masks. This time, I masked up myself and drove them out to the nursing home, feeling pretty good about what I'd done.

That night, maybe due to boredom or just too much time alone with my thoughts, I went onto A2NeighborGram and spilled my guts. I posted about my dress and the masks and the prom cancellation and my new (!!) resolution to make more masks. First come, first served. I hit post and went to get a drink of water.

Less than three minutes later, Jude reached out. His uncle needed as many masks as he could get his hands on for his business.

And I was his gal. Me and my prom dress.

Somewhere along the last week, ever since I messaged him back, Jude-with-the-Danny-Kaye-avatar has become my friend. He likes cats but agrees they're mostly assholes. He likes '80s buddy cop movies but agrees Mel Gibson must be an actual racist if he's racist when he's drunk. He doesn't know how to do his own laundry but admits it's probably easy. He knows about my obsession with *American Famous* and subsequent fangirling over this season's front-runner Judah MacKenzie, but only teases me about it half as much as everyone else does.

And he agrees that Danny Kaye is better than Bing. He says it's only because Bing is rumored to have abused his kids.

Which is a solid reason, I'll give him that.

I check my app again, where Jude's most recent message is waiting for me. I'd messaged him earlier that I was about to cut into the rest of my dress and needed some moral support. I still haven't made the masks I'd promised him, but tonight is the night. Jude was the one to suggest we socially distance-watch *White Christmas* together, as an official farewell to the dress. I'm not sure it's helping.

Gray: You don't understand. It HAS to be this dress.

Gray: If I can't have prom, this is the only acceptable alternative.

Jude: That's fair. Have I told you I'm sorry about your Rosemary Clooney dress?

Jude: Because I am.

Gray: You have. Like twice. So I really need to just suck it up and make the cut.

Jude: It's for a good cause.

Gray: The best cause, yes.

Jude: Would it help if I counted you off?

Gray: It would help more if you were heeeeere.

The honest-to-God truth is that I have zero idea how to talk to boys. Like ZERO. Or at least, I thought that was the case. Turns out, I'm pretty bold when I'm texting during a pandemic, under quarantine when the boy is a total stranger.

Jude: Be right there.

I snicker. We've been talking a week and we've had this conversation six times already.

Gray: Such a tease. You don't even know where I live.

Aside from Ann Arbor, that is, which is a pretty giant college town. Despite being on the neighborhood app, Jude's not from my neighborhood on the west side. Apparently, his uncle is fairly close, but Jude says he goes to one of the other high schools in town, which I happen to know is on the north side.

Well. He *did*. Before COVID-19. Now we're both seniors, just waiting on socially distant graduation ceremonies.

Jude: How about this: send me a picture of the material now, and the material after you make a cut and then the material after you make a mask. It will be like I'm there with you and I can cheer you on.

Gray: Sigh. That's genius.

Jude: Obviously.

I pause the movie, scoot back from my desk, and cross my room to my sewing table in the corner. It's a mess, with itty bitty scraps of the blacker-than-black raw silk I'd skimped and saved for months to buy. Rosemary's dress was rich velvet, but prom is in May and I figured I'd die of heatstroke. A lucky coincidence, since velvet doesn't breathe and raw silk is washable. Not only that, but I did my research and raw silk happens to have special electrostatic properties that make it compatible for very fancy face masks. Also on my table is a sandwich plate covered only in crumbs and two dirty cups with the dregs of cold cinnamon spiced tea staining the bottom. I clear away the debris and take a quick photo of the materials, careful to keep myself out of it. I'm not sure why I don't want Jude to see what I look like. I only know I'm happy in this space where we're relatively anonymous.

I send the pic and sit down at my table, pulling out my sewing shears. One snip. I can do this. It's for a good cause and there will be other dresses. My phone flashes with a notification.

Jude: Excellent. You're going to help so many people.

Jude: I'm so proud of you.

I feel my cheeks heat. Thank goodness he can't see. It's strange. I've only known Jude a little over a week, but it feels like longer. It's so easy to talk to him like this. It's like we skipped over all the awkward small talk and went straight to being close friends. I can't tell if it's because we're online or if it's just Jude and the effect he has on me.

Gray: That's a bit of a stretch.

Jude: Is it? Maybe if it was JUST a dress. But I know it's more than that to you.

Jude: I get it. It sucks.

Jude: You're allowed to think it sucks.

I feel hot tears prickle in the corners of my eyes. It does suck. There are people sick and dying all over the world and I can't leave my house and now I won't ever wear this dress. Things most definitely suck right now.

Gray: Whew.

Jude: Right? So yeah, Gray. I'm proud of you for doing this.

How is he so nice?

Gray: How are you so nice?

Jude: You're the one cutting up your dream dress to make masks for people you've never met. How are YOU so nice?

240

Gray: I'm not sure I am.

Jude: I'm not sure I am either. My younger brother definitely thinks I'm a dick.

Jude: It's easy to be nice to you.

Gray: Your brother and my little sister could start a club.

I'm definitely stalling.

Gray: Okay.

Gray: Okay. I'm going to make some serious cuts now. Thanks for cheering me on!

Jude: You're welcome. Can't wait to see how they turn out!

I toss my phone on my bed behind me, where I can't be distracted by boys with sweet words. I need to concentrate. It's time to make a whole lot of somethings out of nothing and let the magic hum of my sewing machine lull me into my happy place.

—

One week later, I'm finished. No more dress. Just masks. And last night Jude asked what time I'd be dropping off the masks, so he could make sure he was there to meet me.

TO MEET ME.

Now I really wish I'd sent a selfie before this. I'm not nearly as nervous about seeing Jude as I am about Jude seeing me. Which is ridiculous. I'm not usually like that. It's just that I really, *really* like him. Which seems impossible since I've never seen his face and I don't even know what he sounds like, but I know his heart? If that makes sense? Three nights in a row now, we've been up past one a.m. messaging on A2NeighborGram. I know about his family (stupidly in-love parents, annoying younger brother who's a freshman in high school), his favorite foods (barbacoa tacos from Chelas), favorite music (Isak Danielson and Lewis Capaldi), favorite movie (*Beverly Hills Cop*). I know about his hobbies (playing guitar, Call of Duty, and street hockey). I know his goals (college in the fall, performing a song he's written in front of an audience). His fears (school shootings and that his grandpa will catch COVID-19). And I know his history (one quasi-serious high school girlfriend who fell in love with her female best friend . . . things ended amicably).

My phone buzzes with a text. Oh. And that. We exchanged numbers, so we could text all hours.

Jude: Still coming at 10?

Gray: Yep. Packing up the masks now.

Jude: Great! We got a call but I sent my cousin out. I'm determined not to miss you.

Gray: Okay, then. Just remember: I'm the really gorgeous one.

I cringe. What am I saying?

Jude: Obviously.

I grin, relieved.

Gray: That's the spirit.

Gray: See you soon.

I stash my phone in my pocket and give myself a final once-over in the mirror. First time leaving the house this week, so I decided to have fun with it. A pair of skinny-fit denim overalls, cuffed; a bright red tank to celebrate the sunny spring weather; and some carefully applied winged eyeliner. I've got my dark brown hair curled and pulled into a high pony and I've tied a cherry red bandana around it. I slip into my flip-flops and grab another red bandana that I've made into a face mask.

Am I dressed like Rosie the Riveter?

Yes.

Did I coordinate to match my face mask?

You betcha.

You can take the girl out of the costume department, but you can't take the costume department out of the girl.

I grab the box of masks in both hands, wave at my sister who's on the couch watching *Schitt's Creek* again, and am out the door and into the sunshine. It's glorious. The kind of day when I want to drive through for a smoothie, crank some tunes, and tool around Joann Fabrics.

But since that kind of thing isn't allowed, I'll just stick to the music. I turn on some Kacey Musgraves and take some cleansing breaths as I slip on my sunglasses. I can do this. It's just a normal day.

The storefront Jude's uncle rented is in a strip mall. When I pull into the lot, I can see it's the only place with an open door. Everyone else is boarded up for the duration. There's a bookstore on the corner that is doing curbside pickup, but they must have limited hours because the lot is a ghost town. I go around my little Outback, open the trunk, and remove my masks just as another car pulls up, music blaring. A teenaged guy who looks vaguely familiar jumps out, mask on. He's gangly and a little bit soft around the middle. His hair is a brilliant carrot color, sticking out at fuzzy angles, and he's wearing a bright neon tee that says DUBOIS DELIVERY.

I open my mouth to speak, but he cuts me off.

"Gray Archer! The mask queen!"

I squint. "Jude?"

He laughs. "Wrong guy. I'm Colin. I don't know if you remember me. . . . *Seven Brides for Seven Brothers?*"

"Oh, right!" I nod as I suddenly place him. Colin DuBois goes to my high school; he played the lead in the fall musical while I designed costumes and sets. He's got strong vocals and charisma for days, and I'm pretty sure I met his boyfriend at the cast party last fall.

Jude mentioned that he works with his cousin; he must

be related to Colin. Jude *DuBois,* perhaps? Very French. I tuck this potential last name away for secret Google research later.

"Jude! Gray's here!"

My heart leaps up somewhere near my esophagus and I whip around, box of masks in hand, to where another teen-aged guy is standing at the entrance of the store, watching us. I smile and then realize he can't see it. This is weird. Colin gestures for me to follow and I do, keeping a careful six feet of distance between us.

Jude's tall. Really tall. His hair is as dark as mine, with a slight curl that peeks out from underneath his Detroit Tigers cap. His eyes are hidden behind sunglasses and of course his mask is covering the lower half of his face.

I can tell Jude is active; wiry and broad under his neon delivery uniform and khaki shorts. But that's about all I get. I wonder what he's making of my Rosie outfit.

Somehow his entire body seems to smile when he says, "Hi, Gray."

I press my lips together and push my glasses to the top of my head. "Hey, Jude."

Under his mask, I can see his cheeks bulge and I know, I just *know* he's beaming.

"Or should I call you Rosie?"

I shift my box and strike a pose, making a muscle and glancing over my shoulder. "Hell, yes. I'm here to kick some COVID butt."

He laughs, and my heart actually throbs. He has a beautiful laugh. Rich and full and hearty.

I hand him the box, careful to keep my distance. He places it on the table behind him. No accidental (gloved) hand brushes here. No, sir.

"Thank you for these. After the governor made the order for everyone to wear them shopping, a lot of our costumers panicked. You're a lifesaver, literally."

I lift a shoulder and drop my hands into my giant overall pockets. "I'm happy to do it."

Silence stretches between us, but it's not completely awkward. I wonder if it would be too obvious if I pulled down my glasses again, so I can check him out? I definitely feel his gaze on me. I'm tempted to pull out my phone to text him, asking him what he's thinking about.

Colin clears his throat and we both jump. I'd forgotten he was there. "So my dad had a business proposition for you, Gray . . ."

Jude straightens. "Right! I almost forgot! He was wondering if we could commission more masks from you?"

More? My scrap pile is looking rough. I must look skeptical, because Jude keeps talking.

"We'd provide you with materials, obviously."

I raise my eyes to Jude's. Even through the lenses, I can see he's watching me intently.

"Okay. I have plenty of elastic still, but my scrap pile is running low after every person in my family asked for masks, so if you have some fabric . . ."

"We do. I think my uncle got some donations in the back . . ."

"I'll get it," Colin says, giving us a knowing look as he moves past Jude.

As soon as he leaves, Jude exhales and my shoulders slump in relief. Jude laughs again.

"Is it weird that I want to pull out my phone and text you?" he asks in a low voice, his hands tapping out a rhythm on the box in front of him. "I really don't know how to talk to pretty girls."

"How can you even tell?" I wave at my face, hoping he can't see how flushed my cheeks are. "In all this getup."

He leans back, crossing his arms over his chest, and I try not to notice how strong his forearms look. I'm officially a heroine in a Victorian novel, noticing muscular forearms and perfectly proportionate ears, while everything else about his appearance is a mystery.

"I didn't need to see you to be able to tell. But I knew if I told you online, you'd just think I was full of it. As you can see . . ." He trails off awkwardly. "I'm not that smooth."

And he's not. I can't explain how I know, but I know. Maybe it's the old New Balance sneakers or the too-flat brim of his hat. Or the fact that his favorite singers are crooners when every other guy our age is listening to Drake.

But I can tell that he's being genuine, and it makes my stomach do a giddy little flip-flop.

"Thanks," I say. "I didn't need to see you to know you're pretty amazing, too. But it's nice to know you're real."

"You were worried?".

"Maybe not worried," I say. "But I couldn't imagine being that lucky."

"Really?" he asks, sounding so unsure, I practically melt on the spot. I need to leave before I give the middle finger to the CDC and jump across this table to wrap my arms around his waist. This whole thing is equal parts impossible and incredible.

Colin returns and hands me the box of materials. I take it from his outstretched arms and thank him, starting to back away reluctantly. Before I turn to go, I look back at Jude.

"Really, Jude. See you next week."

I can feel his stare as I load the box back into my car and put my seatbelt on. My phone vibrates, and I pull it out.

Jude: I'm the lucky one.

I look up through the windshield and raise my fingertips close to my mask, blowing him a socially distant kiss. Across the lot, he catches it and covers his heart with his palm.

—

"I love Amelia Hargrave in these remote performances," I say over FaceTime to my best friend, Chloe, as our favorite reality show blares in the background. "She seemed a little lost on the main stage back in Hawaii, but she's brilliant in a cozier setting."

On my phone screen, Chloe slips a blond curl behind her ear and purses her lips. "Yeah, I don't think she'd have broken Top Ten if the season had been a normal one. She's just really good at set design. Which"—she pins me with a look—"is probably why you like her. Her vocals are shaky."

"I do love what she does with twinkle lights," I admit.

Chloe and I have been watching *American Famous* together since seventh grade. We might not be in the same room with our bowl of popcorn and chocolate chips between us, but it's nice to have some sense of normalcy. It feels right. Usually the top twenty performances are filmed in some exotic location (this year was Hawaii), but since the pandemic, the competitors are streaming their performances live from their homes. It's strange and interesting. I haven't seen the last two weeks of performances since I was in mask purgatory, but Chloe convinced me this would make me feel better.

She was right.

"So who else is still in?" I ask, crunching loudly on a handful of salted, gooey popcorn.

"What you really want to know is if Judah MacKenzie is still in. Uh-uh," she says, shaking her curls back and forth. "You'll have to wait to find out."

I cross my eyes at her in the screen and settle back into the couch, crossing my legging-clad ankles on the ottoman. During the commercial break, Chloe updates me on her social-distance love life. Just before the pandemic, Ferris Carter, a fellow lead vocalist in show choir, finally asked her to be his girlfriend and prom date. They're currently hovering in the weird place of "serious enough to be official, but not serious enough to break stay-at-home orders to make out."

"I just want to lick his face already," Chloe says, licking her ice cream spoon instead.

I grimace. "Gross."

"Please. Don't even pretend you wouldn't lick Judah MacKenzie's face if you ever had the chance."

"I don't really want to lick anyone's face, ever, and I think it's weird that you do."

"Okay. Maybe that was a little over the top. I just really want to kiss him. A lot. For a long time."

"That's more like it," I say around another mouthful of popcorn, feeling my cheeks burn. Doesn't take much for the hot cheeks these days. Not since meeting Jude in real life, anyway. We spend most of our day talking and flirting via text . . . growing more and more brave. Not brave enough to google him yet, but maybe brave enough to send a maskless selfie.

I casually swipe up on my phone, rereading our conversation.

Gray: Gotta run, American Famous is on in five.

Jude: Don't you mean Judah MacKenzie is on in five?

Jude: I hear he's from Michigan.

Gray: Jealous?

Jude: Maybe a little. Should I be?

Gray: Nah. He's a total Bing. You're definitely a Danny.

Jude: . . .

Jude: You mean you like me for me?

Gray: That's what I'm saying.

Gray: Now shhhh. I need to go fangirl.

The show starts up again and *there he is.*

Judah MacKenzie is standing in the middle of a backyard deck. It's surrounded by pine trees and a hundred softly lit candles, and he looks like every girl's dream. I'm not surprised he's made it this far. He's got gobs of charisma and talent. From the moment he opened his mouth during audition week, I knew he was Final Four material.

I let out a tiny shriek, and Chloe laughs at my blatant fangirling.

He starts off, artfully gazing down at his fingers, plucking away at the opening chords to a song I recognize immediately, my stomach turning a tiny somersault. The thing about Judah MacKenzie is that he's not afraid to experiment, even if it means reimagining an acoustic version of Taylor Swift's "Delicate." Judah raises his face to the light, shaking back his dark waves from his forehead and piercing me with deep-sea-green eyes.

Holy moly, this boy is good-looking.

Everything else falls away. My best friend, popcorn, my house, my existence. All of it, forgotten. I don't dare breathe, can't possibly blink, or I might miss something.

You must like me for me.

"You all right there, Archer?" Chloe says when the song ends.

I blink, shaking my head. "I'm fine. That was amazing."

Chloe giggles. "Cripes, Gray, you were transported there for a minute."

I feel my face get hot. Again. "I love that song."

"Me too! Extra swoony."

Onscreen, the host is making small talk with Judah as the judges gather their thoughts in their own locations and give constructive feedback. I don't follow what they are saying. I just keep hearing his voice in my head. "You must like me for me." Something is niggling in the back of my brain. I narrow my eyes at the boy on my TV. He's tall with dark, wavy hair, bright eyes, and a dimple in his one cheek. I turn up the volume and shush my best friend, who's still giving me shit for drooling into my snack.

But he's done talking. Instead, he's standing in the middle of his deck, holding up eight fingers and miming for us to text and vote.

Which I do. Seventeen times.

I watch the rest of the competitors with Chloe, but I'm distracted. The moment the episode is over, I hang up, telling her I'm tired. After all, I've been staying up late every night sewing masks.

I crawl up the stairs to bed and poke my head in my parents' bedroom, where they're both reading. I blow them a kiss and turn to my own room, fighting the memory of blowing Jude a kiss just the week before.

Jude. I open my texts. He'd said, *You mean you like me for me?*

Jude. Judah. Jude. Judah. Nope. No way. There's no way. I'm making something out of nothing. Yeah, I know Jude plays guitar, but who knows if he can sing? Both guys are from Michigan . . . but so are millions of other people. Both are eighteen-year-old seniors in high school. Again, not super unique.

I would know if the guy I've been talking to almost non-stop was a celebrity.

Right?

I pull up Google and press my lips together, taking a deep breath before typing "Jude DuBois + Michigan" in the search field. I scroll through the results, but there's not much. A few hits on his uncle's delivery service. A link to Colin's social media. But nothing else. Either Jude has zero social media presence or DuBois isn't actually his last name.

Frustrated, I look up Judah MacKenzie's Instagram account. It pops up immediately. A million followers, blue check mark. For a reality show contestant, he seems to do the bare minimum. Just photos of him performing from his back porch, and back in Hawaii on the set of *American Famous* before the pandemic. I try YouTube. Same story there. Besides, I already know what Judah looks and sounds like. I try to hold my hand over his face on the screen and squint my eyes . . . if I imagine a pair of sunglasses just like . . .

Forget it. I close out of the page with a sigh. There is zero evidence to suggest Jude and Judah are the same person.

But there's also zero evidence they *aren't* the same person.

I check our text history. We don't usually talk on Sunday nights, which could be because he's performing live from his backyard for millions of viewers.

Or it could be a million other logical reasons.

I think about texting him now, but what on earth should I say? *Hey, Jude, you aren't actually Judah MacKenzie, mega-hot contestant on American Famous, are you? No? Oh. Okay. I was just wondering.*

Better not.

The next morning, I wake up to a buzzing on my night stand. I pull my phone toward me and smile.

Jude: I got Doris Day. Who are you? *attachment BuzzWord Quiz WHICH HOLLYWOOD IT GIRL ARE YOU?*

Jude: I'm predicting Grace Kelly.

Gray: Wow, no pressure there!

Jude: Just calling it like I see it.

Gray: Okay, okay. Gimme a sec.

Gray: I just woke up.

I hesitate and then decide to drop the tiniest nugget.

Gray: Was up late watching American Famous.
Popcorn hangover.

I watch the gray dots with a nervous feeling in my stomach.

Jude: I bet you look really cute when you first wake
up. Hair all over. Puffy eyes.

I release my breath. Okay. Well, that was uneventful (and
massively sweet). Fine.

Gray: We have very different definitions of the word "cute."

I click through BuzzWord, answering the quiz, while
propped up on my pillow.

Gray: Hey! You were right. I got Princess Grace Kelly!

Jude: Knew it.

Deciding to be bold, I lift my phone over my head, making
sure to capture every glorious hair out of place, snap the fuzzy
selfie, and hit send.

Gray: You mean you like me for me?

Jude: That's what I'm saying.

—

JUDE

In my defense, I was wearing a mask. I had to. It was required by the law and also my uncle. So I wasn't trying to hide my identity. I never lied.

In fact, I was more truthful than I've ever been in my whole life.

That's the thing about a mask. It allows you to be realer than real because you don't have to be you. The you that everyone else knows, carefully cultivated over years of trial and error.

But I'm getting ahead of myself. The first time I saw Gray Archer was earlier this year, at the cast party for my cousin Colin's musical. Last fall. Before any of *gestures at the world* this. Before the *American Famous* audition where I was only supposed to be accompanying Colin but ended up making it into the Top Ten. Before the millions of hits on my barely existent YouTube channel. Before the girls flooding the comment sections and texting to vote for me week after week.

Before the pandemic brought the entire world to a screaming, screeching halt.

Before all of that, I was just a guy nursing a breakup at a rival high school's theater department after party. Colin had dragged me along, insisting I needed to stop moping, and then promptly ditched me at the door to accept his accolades and show off his boyfriend. Typical Colin. And I ended up spending the entire night warming a couch cushion in a basement, surrounded by strangers.

It wasn't that bad, honestly. Better than being home, watching my little brother play Xbox with his friends. And it's where I first met her.

It was barely a blip on her radar, I know, but I won't forget it. She sat next to me on that couch for over an hour, talking animatedly with her friends about the glory days of Hollywood costume design, and debating whether *To Catch a Thief* or *High Society* showcased Grace Kelly's best looks. At one point, she waved her hands so wildly, she smacked me in the head. When she apologized, I held out my hand and introduced myself.

"It's okay. You were on a roll. I'm Jude."

She smiled, full on, and shook my hand. "I'm Gray." Then she immediately turned to finish her argument.

So I sat and listened and watched and fell under the spell of this girl. That was it. You don't forget a name like Gray and you don't forget a girl like Gray Archer. But that night, I went home and never saw her again.

After that, my life got pretty crazy. I created a public Instagram account that immediately earned a blue check. I finished my senior year through a tutor. I spent January in Hawaii taping the top twenty episodes for *American Famous*. And I'm grateful. This is my dream.

But when I logged on to my uncle's A2NeighborGram

account and saw Gray's post, it was like the world's strongest magnet drawing me to her. I just wanted to be her friend.

Maybe more.

Please, please, please let her still want me when she knows who I am.

GRAY

Jude: Are you watching American Famous tonight?

Gray: Duh. Chloe would disown me if I didn't. I missed two weeks in a row because of mask making and she threatened to replace me with her boyfriend, Ferris.

Jude: Not Ferris.

Gray: I know right?

Jude: Girls before Tilt-a-Whirls

Gray: Um

Gray: What?

Jude: Sorry

Jude: Ferris -> Ferris wheel -> Tilt-a-Whirl

Gray: That was rough, man.

Jude: You still like me.

Gray: Lord help me I do.

Gray: This is going to sound very awkward, but.

Jude: Yes?

Jude: Sorry! I have to run!

Gray: What is your last name?

I stare at my screen, confused for a second. We must have messaged each other at the same time, and now Jude's gone. I glance up at my clock. It's nearly eight. Time for *American Famous.*

At the mask dropoff yesterday, I stayed nearly thirty minutes, talking with Jude alone, while Colin did deliveries. It was heaven. Muffled heaven. Because, yes, I was doing everything in my power to study and memorize his voice. Maybe I don't have a solid idea of how Jude sounds, but I definitely know how he talks. How he leans forward and uses his hands when he's excited about something. How he throws his head back and his entire face scrunches when he laughs. How the tips of his perfect ears and back of his neck redden when he's embarrassed.

Like when Colin came back early from a delivery and said to me, "You know this is his favorite part of the week, don't you? It's all he talks about. *When Gray comes* this . . . and *when Gray comes by* that . . . You'd think the guy had nothing else going on."

"Well," I said with a shrug, feeling warm, but pleased, "It's a pandemic. What else *does* he have going on?"

Before Colin could respond, Jude cleared his throat and said, "Yeah. Well. You get to see your boyfriend practically every day when you"—he does air quotes—"*deliver his lunch,* so excuse me for savoring my one visit a week."

That's right, he basically called me his girlfriend. Sort of. Practically.

Chloe FaceTimes me at exactly 7:59, and I smile at her flushed pink face.

"Almost missed it," she says.

"How is that possible? We're stuck at home."

She rolls her eyes. "Mel is having a fit because I made her switch over from *USA's Funniest Stay at Home Videos*. It's all the same garbage we've seen on social media all day every day. They're basically ripping off TikTok and featuring a bunch of influencers. Not interested."

"Right, well it's on now. So shush."

"Oh, there he is, Gray! Is it him?"

I had to tell someone my theory about Jude and Judah maybe possibly being the same person. Chloe was the least humiliating option.

"I don't know! I need to hear him speak. I might be able to tell from that."

"I can't believe you didn't just ask him."

"I wanted to, but it felt weird. Like what if it's not and then he thinks I'm disappointed he's not a celebrity? That would be soul-crushing."

"You think?"

"What if he was obsessed with Dove Cameron or something and thought I was her, and then found out I was just me? Wouldn't that feel terrible?"

"I guess. But you won't be disappointed if he's not some celeb."

"*I* know that, but *he* doesn't. I really, really like Jude. So much."

"All right. Just so we're clear, are we hoping its him, or aren't we?"

"We're ambivalent."

"Really?"

"Mostly."

"Right."

"Quiet, it's starting," I say. "I'm still sad what's-her-face got voted off last week."

"So sad that you can't be bothered to remember her name."

"Good point."

I've barely touched my popcorn. If only Jude hadn't had to run off earlier, I would already know if my crazy theory were true! I can't believe I don't know his last name. What kind of girl doesn't know her maybe-boyfriend's last name?

The kind who meets him in a pandemic, that's who.

I'm my own antagonist.

"He's next after the break," Chloe says in a hissed whisper.

I wipe my hands down my black leggings and take a deep, cleansing breath.

It doesn't really matter. I might not even be able to tell. And that's okay. He knows I'm watching tonight. Maybe I can bring it up again, casually and—

Oh God. He's on. It's the same back porch, with the same evergreens, but this time its covered in blue and green twinkle lights. His back is facing the camera, but he spins, doing this kind of slow reveal, and I let out a high-pitched shriek.

He's wearing my mask. The one I made for him from my prom dress.

Oh my word, it's HIM.

IT'S JUDE.

He's standing in front of a mic stand, mask in place, and it's then that I hear the song that's playing. He tugs off the mask, tucking it into his jacket pocket. A jacket that looks like it's black velvet. His mic is one of those giant old-fashioned ones, and the song? It's "Love, You Didn't Do Right by Me" by Rosemary Clooney.

"Is it him?" Chloe screams.

All I can do is nod.

"Holy crap!"

I watch the entire performance, my face hot in my hands, and my heart in my throat. He's so good-looking and so sweet and he's mine. Judah MacKenzie is my Jude. And he's singing me a song on TV.

When the song wraps, he pulls something out of his pocket, and with a secretive smile, he pulls it over his face. Another mask. This one with a message written across the front.

It says I CAN BE YOUR DANNY KAYE.

Sweet Jesus.

"I have to go there," I say to my best friend once I've finished screaming internally.

"Hell yes, you do. Where is that exactly?"

I gesture wildly at the television screen in front of me. "There! *There!* To his house! I have to go there and see him and tell him I want him to be my Danny Kaye!"

She rolls her eyes on the screen. "Right. I know. I got that. *Everyone* got that, but Gray. *Where* is his house?"

Oh my gosh, I have no idea. Jude lives in Ann Arbor, but so do a hundred thousand other people.

I surge from the couch and shout at the phone between my shaking hands. "I need Colin DuBois's phone number. Do you still have the theater department phone tree?"

"Yeah. Hanging right here next to me. I'll snap you a pic."

"Okay. I'll call him and beg for Jude's address. And . . ." I take a deep, calming breath. "And I'm going to put on real pants. And then I'm gonna tell him how I feel."

"Quarantine!" my best friend reminds me.

"Right. I'll just have to get creative." My mind is already whirring with possibilities. I can think of something on the way.

"Good luck! I love you! Call me later!"

I hang up and sprint up the stairs to my room to change. I pull on a pair of skinny jeans and pull down my hair, brushing out the waves and spritzing perfume like an optimist. Chloe sends over the screenshot of Colin's phone number and it takes me two tries to put the numbers into my phone. He answers on the first ring.

"Colin! This is—"

"Gray Archer!"

I'm caught off guard. "How'd you know?"

"I put your name in my phone after the musical. Never know when you'll need a tailor."

"Oh! Right. Thank you." I shake my head. "Um. Anyway, it's him, isn't it? Jude is Judah?"

"Ah. You watched."

"Of course I watched! I *always* watch! I need to get over there. Can you send me his address?"

"I knew that Danny Kaye thing had to be something

between you two. So mysterious. Already the interwebs are aflutter with speculation . . ."

"Colin. Focus. Address."

"Calm down, Lover Girl. I'm sending it now."

I hang up and tap on my parents' door. "Is it okay if I take a little drive? I've got my hand sanitizer and mask."

"No stores," my mom reminds me.

"Cross my heart."

I'm in the car and reversing out of my drive in an instant, still not entirely sure what I'm going to do. My eyes graze the clock and I realize with a start that it's barely 8:45. *American Famous* is still on. Jude is still in his backyard for the live shots. I slow down, but he doesn't live that far. I pull into his neighborhood just minutes after nine, but when Siri tells me I've arrived, I drive past his house. I'm too scared to pull up. It takes me twice more around the block before I pull in.

I get a text from Colin, my ultimate wingman.

Colin: His bedroom is the front, right, second story with the balcony.

Holy poop, I can't believe I'm going to do this.

I reach into the backseat and grab a cardboard box, left over from my face mask deliveries. I pull it apart to create a square. On the board, I write a message.

For a minute, hot panic surges in my chest. What if his performance *wasn't* for me? What if the whole mask–*White Christmas*–Danny Kaye thing was just a coincidence?

265

Welp. Then I guess I'll just have to change my name and disappear forever. I don't have time to worry about that right now.

I pull my car forward, directly under the streetlight outside his balcony. I reallllly hope Colin's not messing with me.

I pull out my phone and scroll through all my playlists for a song. I find one I've had on repeat every day for a week. "Delicate" by Taylor Swift. It's kind of dramatic to play him his own song, but so is this entire gesture that I'm attempting. Go for broke. Desperate times call for desperate measures, and it doesn't get more desperate than a worldwide pandemic.

Plus, it's kind of perfect for us. *You must like me for me* is really hitting home, now that I know his secret. And I really, really *do* like him.

I glance up at the window and see it's lit. Opening my messages app, I type:

Gray: Hey Romeo, come to your balcony!

I'm staring at the curtains at his window when he pulls them aside and pokes his head out.

I open all the windows and my door, turn my stereo all the way up, and hit play.

Then I reach for my sign and stand with it raised over my head in the streetlight, my face burning but unmasked. I watch him climb out onto his balcony. In my periphery, I can see more lights turn on, probably everyone in the neighborhood wondering who's blaring Taylor Swift, but I ignore them, singularly focused on his handsome face. His full beaming smile, dimple and sparkling eyes, all for me, as he reads my sign: *I DON'T NEED DANNY, I JUST WANT YOU.*

He looks so happy.

I made him that way.

My phone buzzes in my pocket and he gestures over the blaring music with his in his hand.

Jude: You have me if you want me. I'm just Jude, though. Just the guy from the texts.

Gray: That's all I want. Just Jude.

Jude: Just Jude and Just Gray.

Jude: I wish I could kiss you.

I hold up a finger, reaching back in the car for a receipt. I write on it:

IOU One Hell of a First Kiss and I crumple it up in a ball, tossing it up to him on the balcony. He opens it, grins, and tucks it into his jacket pocket. The song ends and the silence is so loud. All these things we aren't used to saying in person, ringing in the air between us.

"I have to go," I say.

He nods in the soft yellow light. "Quarantine won't last forever," he says.

"I know. I can wait for you. You're worth it, Jude."

"Until then?" He holds up his phone.

"Until then." I blow him a kiss. Then I pick up my sign, get in my car, and drive home.

And that night, before I fall asleep, I cast a thousand votes for my boyfriend, Jude MacKenzie. He's earned every single one.

ABOUT THE AUTHORS

Erin A. Craig is the *New York Times* bestselling author of the *House of Salt and Sorrows*. She has always loved telling stories. After getting her BFA in theater design and production from the University of Michigan, she stage-managed tragic operas filled with hunchbacks, séances, and murderous clowns, then decided she wanted to write books that were just as spooky. An avid reader, a decent quilter, a rabid basketball fan, and a collector of typewriters, Erin makes her home in West Michigan with her husband and daughter.

erinacraig.com
@Penchant4Words on Twitter and Instagram

Auriane Desombre is a former English teacher currently pursuing an MA in English lit at New York University and an MFA in creative writing for children at the New School in New York. *I Think I Love You* is her debut novel.

aurianedesombre.com
@AurianeDesombre on Twitter

Erin Hahn is the author of *You'd Be Mine* and *More Than Maybe*. She teaches elementary school, would rather be outside, and makes a lot of playlists. So many playlists, in fact, that she decided to write books to match them! She married her very own YA love interest, whom she met on her first day of college, and has two kids who are much, much cooler than she ever was at their age. She lives in Ann Arbor, Michigan, aka the greenest place on earth, and has a cat named Gus who plays fetch and a dog named June who doesn't.

erinphahn.com
@erinhahn_author on Twitter and Instagram

© Alyson Derrick

Rachael Lippincott is the number one *New York Times* best-selling author of *Five Feet Apart*. She holds a BA in English writing from the University of Pittsburgh. Originally from Bucks County, Pennsylvania, she lives in Pittsburgh with her wife and their dog, Hank.

rachaellippincott.com
@rachaellippincott on Instagram

Bill Konigsberg is the award-winning author of six young adult novels, including *The Bridge*. In 2018, the National Council of Teachers of English (NCTE)'s Assembly on Literature for Adolescents (ALAN) established the Bill Konigsberg Award for Acts and Activism for Equity and Inclusion Through Young Adult Literature. Prior to turning his attention to writing books for teens, Bill was a sports writer and editor for the Associated Press and ESPN.com. He lives in Phoenix, Arizona, with his husband, Chuck, and their Australian Labradoodles, Mabel and Buford.

billkonigsberg.com

© Kariba Jack Photography

Brittney Morris is the bestselling author of *SLAY*. She holds a BA in economics from Boston University because back then, she wanted to be a financial analyst. (She's now thankful that didn't happen.) She spends her spare time reading, playing indie video games, and enjoying the rain from her house in Philadelphia. She lives with her husband, Steven, who would rather enjoy the rain from a campsite in the woods because he hasn't played enough horror games. Brittney is the founder and former president of the Boston University Creative Writing Club, and she's a four-time NaNoWriMo winner.

authorbrittneymorris.com
@BrittneyMMorris on Twitter and Instagram

Sajni Patel was born in vibrant India and raised in the heart of Texas, surrounded by lots of delicious food and plenty of diversity. She draws on her personal experiences, cultural expectations, and Southern flair to create worlds that center on strong Indian women. Once an MMA fighter, she's now all about puppies and rainbows and tortured love stories. She lives in Austin, where she not-so-secretly watches Matthew McConaughey from afar during UT football games. Queso is her weakness, and thanks to her family's cooking, Indian/Tex-Mex cuisine is a real thing. She's a die-hard Marvel Comics fan and a lover of chocolates from around the world, and she is always wrapped up in a story.

sajnipatel.com
@SajniPatelBooks on Twitter and Instagram

© Gavin Smith

Natasha Preston is the #1 *New York Times* bestselling author of *The Cellar, The Cabin, Awake, You Will Be Mine, The Lost,* and her latest novel, *The Twin.* A UK native, she discovered her love of writing when she shared a story online—and she hasn't looked back. She enjoys writing romance, thrillers, gritty YA, and the occasional serial killer.

natashapreston.com
@AuthorNPreston on Twitter
@authornatashapreston on Instagram

Jennifer Yen is a Taiwanese American author who lives with her adorable dog in Texas. She spends her days healing the hearts of others and her nights writing about love, family, and the power of acceptance. Jennifer believes in the magic of imagination, and she hopes her stories will bring joy and inspiration to readers. Her debut novel is *A Taste for Love*. If you find her wandering around aimlessly, please return her to the nearest milk tea shop.

jenyenwrites.com
@JenYenWrites on Twitter and Instagram